FLAMINGO
BOOK OF NEW SCOTTISH
WRITING
1998

FLAMINGO
BOOK OF NEW SCOTTISH WRITING
1998

Flamingo
An Imprint of HarperCollins*Publishers*

THE SCOTTISH ARTS COUNCIL

Flamingo
An Imprint of HarperCollins*Publishers*
77–85 Fulham Palace Road,
Hammersmith, London w6 8jb

Published by Flamingo 1998
9 8 7 6 5 4 3 2 1

The Publisher acknowledges the financial assistance of the
Scottish Arts Council in the publication of this volume

A catalogue record for this book is
available from the British Library

isbn o oo 655118 1

Set in Postscript Linotype New Baskerville by
Rowland Phototypesetting Ltd,
Bury St Edmunds, Suffolk

Printed and bound in Great Britain by
Clays Ltd, St Ives plc

CONTENTS

FLAMINGO
BOOK OF NEW SCOTTISH
WRITING
1998

THE INITIATION

Laura J. Hird

The fog was sliceably thick and clung to them like wet clothes. A thin coat of condensation covered the park bench so that she and Jackie had to squeeze their bums together on the carrier bag they'd got the fags and juice in. Even the leaves and grass were damp although it hadn't rained for days. Lighting the first two Regals from the ten-pack they stared in silence through their smoky breath as ghostly shapes dodged in and out the swirling pyramids of light above the tennis courts – jogging, walking dogs, running to and from unknown destinations.

They laughed as a patch of sky above St Michael's kindled with a bang, reminding of Miss Bennett's white, scared face that afternoon. A fortnight had passed since Guy Fawkes Night but the smells and sounds of treason lingered.

'A still cannae get over that shakin',' mused Jackie, sympathetically. 'She's had bennies before, like but that was ootrageous. Single fare to the Andrew Duncan job.' She feigned an epileptic seizure for full effect.

Claire echoed her friend's hilarity but felt a private pity for their teacher. Setting the firework off in the classroom had raised her several notches in the estimation of the bullies she wanted so hard to impress, but something niggled her. When they'd seen Miss Bennett afterwards through the headmaster's door, crying hysterically and that weird trembling it was like she'd completely lost control. Claire knew she was responsible, though anonymously, for getting an adult in such a state and it made her feel great but awful at the same time.

Claire watched her friend sucking on a Regal as she rocked backwards and forwards on the bench, hugging herself, smiling into the fog.

'It was a cracker, Claire! Maybe there's hope for yi yet.'

The slight accolade evaporated Claire's doubts and made her feel gloriously hard.

'It served her right. Fucking old bag,' she spat, relishing the feel of the bad word on her lips.

Jackie guffawed, repeating her friend's words in pigeon posh.

'Sorry, like. It jist sounds funny when you say it, ken?'

Claire held the cigarette out in front of her, thinking how pale and lovely her hand looked in this light – almost like a statue. Jackie stamped her cigarette into the grass, then quickly dropped her head towards her friend and whispered an order.

'Hoi! Look down. Pretend you havnae seen him!'

'Seen who?' said Claire predictably as a tall, gangly youth shambled out of the gloom, grinning vacantly.

'Shite!' muttered Jackie.

The boy now loomed over them, beaming down, hands plunged deep into jogging bottoms.

'Whit yi up ti, girls? It's a stinkin' night.'

Jackie scrutinized her shoes. Claire knew she had to get rid of him.

4

'We're having a gang meeting. We've got important things to talk about.'

The boy slumped down beside her, excited.

'A gang! A didnae ken yi wur in a gang, Jackie.'

Jackie looked at Claire and shrugged, willing her to elaborate on the lie and get rid of him.

'Whit gang's this then? Whit's it called?' he persisted, nudging Claire to respond.

She desperately clutched at a name she'd seen sprayed on a few bus stops.

'The SWP. You better not tell anyone though.'

The boy gaped at them, his mouth hanging open, vaporizing in the cold air.

'You must have seen it. It's written all over the place.'

He smiled, not really registering, and looked at her friend.

'Aye, brilliant, Jackie. It must be brilliant been in u big gang. Ad love that. It must be brilliant.'

'Aye, Johnnie, it's brilliant,' said Jackie, reluctantly looking up from her shoes. 'Will yi leave us alone now?'

Johnnie stood up, embarrassed, and shoogled his crotch.

'Aye, awright girls. Al away likes. Brilliant aboot yir gang, though.'

But he didn't go away. He stood, shuffling awkwardly, hopping on one foot then the other, clearing his throat nervously.

'See ya then,' Jackie shouted.

Johnnie shut his eyes, screwed up his face and put his hands on his head. He let out a whine. Claire felt a less subtle approach might work.

'Look, will you fuck off!'

Johnnie ignored her, pointing behind them at the

5

canal. His eyes remained shut as he continued his long, high-pitched wailing.

'What the fuck . . .' hissed Jackie. 'You're doing my head in.'

He began hopping again, still pointing towards the water.

'Mah hoose. Hiv yir meetin' in ma hoose. Yi cannae sit oot here.'

They both looked around but could only see the faint outline of the canal bank through the fog. Jackie looked back at Johnnie, gyrating on the grass to the sound of his own whining.

'A thought yi wir stayin' in the hospital. Wi cannae have oor meetin' in there.'

Her words seemed to please him.

'Naw, naw, no any more. They said A kid go. Thir wisnae enough room for ais.'

'What about your mum?' asked Claire, slightly intrigued. Johnnie laughed as if she'd said something ridiculous.

'Nah, A cannae see her causey ma thievin'. A cannae help it like. A jist dinnae think. A kin git yi stuff though, fir yir gang like. Biscuits, juice. If yi use ma hoose Al make sure yi have biscuits.'

Jackie held up the packet of Regals.

'What aboot them? Kin yi get us them?'

Johnnie nodded his head enthusiastically and began jiving backwards towards the canal, beckoning them.

'Aye. C'mon. A kin git anything. That Paki disnae watch. He's ayewis on the phone.'

They followed him without really knowing why. He skipped across the bridge and disappeared through the gate at the other side. They climbed through after him, emerging on the steps that led to the boatshed. He was missing in the fog.

'Johnnie?'

'Aye, c'mon. It's jist doon here.'

Claire wondered if this was what her mother meant about not going away with strange men. Johnnie was certainly strange, and a man, in his twenties at least, but he just had the brain of a wee boy. He just wanted to be their friend. It was sort of exciting now too. She grabbed Jackie by the arm and they hurried down the steps after him. He stood proudly beside a little dirty hut at the side of the boatshed.

'Wow, don't you get scared here?' asked Jackie, thinking the place looked like something out of a video nasty.

'Scared i what? Am no scared.'

'You're no scared i anythin', ur yi Johnnie?' winked Jackie.

'No really. A dinnae like being' high up, mind. That makes me feel a bit funny but no really. Am no scared.'

Claire found it hard to believe. The shed was so overgrown she probably wouldn't have noticed it if it hadn't been pointed out to her. A wonderful place for a gang hut, though. If only they had a gang.

Johnnie pushed the hingeless door to the side, they walked in and he pulled it partly over the doorway again. He switched on a strip light on the wall. Jackie lit a cigarette as Claire nosed around. It was pretty disgusting. A pishy mattress and ancient sleeping bag took up most of the space. What floor there was was littered with half-eaten tins of food, boxes, plastic bags, sweetie wrappers, various pages of newspapers and dirty magazines. Claire stared at a photo of a woman with her hand between her legs. It was funny-looking. Her fanny looked like an overripe tomato that had burst and she had even fewer pubes than Claire did.

Johnnie was telling Jackie about things he could steal for them as she sat on the mattress and scanned his lovely home.

'Yid have ti tidy it up though. Before we could use it, like. If yi kin git us they ciggies though, that'd be great.'

Johnnie bounded about, offering them both biscuits, giggling, trying to show them things.

'Oh A will, A will. Al enjoy doin' it fir our gang. I've nivir been in a gang before.'

Jackie looked at Claire.

'Who said yi wir in oor gang? Yi cannae be in oor gang jist like that. Yi can git us the biscuits an fags, like, but that's jist so we use this place fir oor meetin's.'

Claire sat on the mattress beside her friend. Johnnie started dancing around and whining again. Claire thought he might be quite nice looking if he wasn't a retard. Jackie held her ears.

'Stop that fucking racket will yi Johnnie? Go ootside u minute and we'll see if we kin let yi in the gang.'

He hopped expectantly. She pointed at the door and he left them alone.

'OK then. You started all this gang shite. Whit d' we tell him? Ad sooner sit here at night than freeze ma knackers off in the park or some shitey shop doorway, like.'

Jackie was right. They needed a proper place to go at nights. Neither of their houses was any good. Jackie came from a large Catholic family and shared a room with two of her wee brothers. Claire's was no good as her mum didn't like her hanging around with Jackie's lot anyway as her family were never out of trouble with the police. This place could soon be done up, in fact, Johnnie would probably beg to do it for them. All this and free fags! And all they had to do was convince him there was a gang. He was so easy to fool they could play it by ear. It would be a right laugh. They could have him eating out of their hands, and he'd supply the biscuits.

Jackie shouted outside for Johnnie to come in. He greeted them as if they were long-lost friends and immediately started dancing around excitedly, tracing invisible patterns in the air with his hands. The two girls sat together on the mattress like Mafiose.

They'd agreed that Claire do the talking to start off with since the gang had been her idea.

'OK, Johnnie, we've had a wee talk and we're going to let you do three sort of tests before we can let you in the gang.'

'Whit? Like gettin' yir biscuits?' asked Johnnie, trying unsuccessfully to curb his excited dancing.

'An fags', added Jackie.

Claire took control again.

'No. The stealing thing you have to do anyway. That's going to be your gang role. Just like you have to keep this place clean for us.'

Johnnie's movements became less frenetic as he tried to concentrate on her words. He crouched on the floor beside them.

'Aye, A ken, A ken. Jist tellies whit ti dae, like.'

Jackie looked on with amusement as Claire continued.

'Right then, it's best if you do the three tests tonight,

so you can start sorting this place out when we're at school tomorrow.'

'Aye, aye. Awe. This is brilliant. A cannae believe it,' he shrieked, jumping up and down on his haunches, clapping like a hysterical Cossack.

'OK then. First we'll have to see if you're fit enough to be in the gang. OK. So you'll have to take your clothes off so we can check you.'

Jackie clucked in disbelief. Johnnie seemed to think this was a marvellous idea, however, which hadn't really been Claire's intention. He pulled off his T-shirt, sweatshirt and jogging top in one enthusiastic lump then started on his bottom half. They both looked on dumbstruck. Johnnie's breathing was heavy and excited. As the trousers passed his hips they gawped at the outline of his willie through the brown nylon Y-fronts. It was gigantic, so big it stuck out the top of his pants. Claire let out a shriek of disgusted glee. Jackie almost choked with laughter, hiding her head behind Claire's back.

'Dinnae, dinnae, Al be sick. Make him put it away!'

When they finally managed to curb their laughter and looked up again, Johnnie had taken his pants down and was standing tickling himself. Claire put one hand over her eyes, and waved the other in front of him.

'No, Johnnie, it's all right. That'll do now. Honest. You're really fi . . .'

Her words subsided into renewed hysterics as Johnnie pulled his trousers back up. Jackie fanned her chest melodramatically and rolled her eyes.

'Aye, right, Johnnie. Very good. Yill hiv ti show it to Claire on her own sometime though. She'd like that.'

They exploded again and wrestled each other on to

the floor as Johnnie stood smiling nervously, rubbing his chest. Jackie surfaced from the scrum first and held her hand up to get attention.

'Right, right. I'll do the next one. OK.'

Claire giggled back on to the mattress. She'd already thought of another task but she'd let Jackie go first. Johnnie was on his haunches again and she could still see the outline of the big hard thing in his trousers which made her feel pretty and powerful. Jackie was taking centre stage now.

'Ok, the next thing is yiv goat ti get the gang name tattooed on yi so folk ken yir in the gang.'

Johnnie looked worried.

'Bit A cannae afford a tattoo. They cost loads, do they no?'

'Aye, loads an loads, an yi cannae just walk out withoot paying cithcr.'

Johnnie looked increasingly upset as his membership of the gang seemed to slip away from him again.

'Bit A cannae afford it,' he droned.

'A ken, A ken,' said Jackie, trying to stop him making that awful noise again, 'dinnae worry aboot money. Yi hiv ti do it yersell anyway.'

'Ooooh,' shrieked Claire in delight at her friend's disgusting new idea. Johnnies big daft mouth hung open as he tried to make sense of it all.

'OK. D'yi hiv a knife or summat. Summat wi' a sharp point?'

Claire bit her bottom lip in delight. She was feeling almost ecstatic with the badness of it all.

Johnnie was shaking his head, looking a bit over-whelmed. Jackie crawled across the room and picked up an open tin with its lid still attached then dropped it and came back over with a rusty tin opener, the type with the spike. Johnnie looked warily at the vicious-looking weapon in her hand.

'It'll hurt, will it no?'

'It's supposed ti hurt. That's why yi do it. If yi want in the gang yiv got ti be able ti take a wee bit pain.'

She handed him the tin opener.

'Just write "SWP" on yir arm. Quite deep so yi git a good scar.'

His mouth dropped open again.

'A dinnae ken whit that looks like.'

'S . . . W . . . P,' Jackie sniped, as if she were talking to a child. He was a child.

'A ken, A ken, but A dinnae ken whit that looks like,' he shrieked, agitated now. 'A cannae read.'

Jackie tutted disgustedly and asked Claire for a pen.

'There's one in there,' said Johnnie, timidly pointing at a cardboard box next to the mattress.

Claire crawled over to the box, rummaged around and pulled out the pen and some drawings. They were in blue biro of the canal, the park, Johnnie's room.

'Did you do these?'

Johnnie looked round to see what she was talking about then ran over and grabbed them off her.

'Please dinnae look at these, thir secret.'

Claire pushed him away, 'Don't wet yourself, I'm only looking.'

Johnnie relented but still took the drawings from her and put them back in the box. Jackie drummed her fingers on her thigh.

'Look, just bring the fuckin' pen o'er here, will yi? We dinnae want ti see yi fuckin' drawin's anyway. No secrets though, right?'

Johnnie cowered over, offered her his arm and looked away.

'Am no doin' it fir yi! Al write it oan in pen and yi kin trace it. Yi kin manage that, surely.'

She smirked at Claire, pointing at him and pulling faces behind his back, then slowly began writing in large blue letters down the side of his arm,

'I . . . AM . . . A . . . SHITE'.

Claire started laughing again. Why were horrible things so funny? Jackie sat back and admired her artwork then picked the tin opener off the floor and handed it to Johnnie.

'Right, jist trace o'er that. Deep as A said.'

Johnnie began scratching at the first 'I'. Jackie stopped him.

'No, Johnnie, it his tae be a lot deeper thin that. It his tae bleed or yi winnae git a decent scar.'

He winced as he pushed a few millimetres of the spike into his flesh and let out a little squeal. The girls watched on, fascinated.

'An nae noise. Yi hiv tae show us how brave yi are.'

The top of the 'I' was bloody and brown from the rust on the tin opener. There were several breaks in the cut but it was still legible. As he continued, he had to keep wiping the blood from his arm so he could see the pen marks.

The girls were silent. Johnnie was determined but slow. His tongue stuck out between his teeth as he squinted at the deepening scar, breathing heavily in concentration. He had no look of pain any more, just the will to carry on. To please them.

At last he finished and wiped away some of the blood with his saliva on a bit of newspaper. They all admired it. The breaks in the lines gave it a jagged, barbed-wire look that was quite effective. Claire felt a bit guilty but still found it funny as she watched Johnnie staring down proudly at the words, 'I am a shite', sliced into his skinny arm.

Jackie stood up, moved the door and told them to come outside. She told Claire to run earth into Johnnie's arm to stain the scar. The idea disgusted Claire but she didn't want to look like a coward so she led Johnnie outside. Yucking and screwing up her face, she pressed the soil into the gashes on his arm. Johnnie barely reacted as he was still transfixed by his new tattoo. When Jackie told her to stop she rushed over to the canal bank and frantically washed the dirt and blood from her hands, thinking about his next task. Yes, Jackie would love this one. She walked back over to them both.

'OK, Johnnie. Just one more thing you have to do tonight. Then you've passed the first stage to be in the gang.'

They all went back into the hut and she told him about the episode with the teacher and the firework that afternoon. They both hated the teacher as she'd tried to get Jackie expelled for getting into fights all the time. Johnnie told Jackie she was like his sister whom he didn't see any more and he didn't like anyone who tried to hurt her. Claire said that the teacher some-times hit Jackie and gave her bad marks just so she'd fail all the time. Johnnie started crying as they embroidered wilder and wilder lies about the schoolteacher.

Eventually Johnnie couldn't listen any more he was so upset. He put his arms up over his eyes and sobbed. To block them out he put his fingers in his ears but he still sobbed. He hated the teacher too for the way she'd treated Jackie. He'd never met her but he hated her. He told them he had to go out to do the toilet, to be on his own for a few minutes. As he picked up some newspaper from the floor to wipe himself with, Claire grabbed him by the wrist.

'No, wait, Johnnie. Don't waste it.'

He froze, rigid in her grip, scared of what they were going to make him do next.

'You want to get your own back on that teacher, don't you?'

Johnnie looked worried.

'For what she's done to Jackie? You do love Jackie, don't you?'

He was getting all confused and anxious again and was having trouble speaking. A little squeak was all he could muster.

'You want to stop her being horrible, don't you?'

He began sobbing again.

'A want ti help. A really do. I want ti be in the gang an all but A dinnae want ti hurt anyone. Yi gonti make me hurt her.'

Claire put her hand on his shoulder, trying to calm him.

'No we're not. Not hurt her. Just give her a bit of a fright.'

He was wailing. 'Naw, naw, I winnae hurt anyone.'

Claire was getting impatient. He wouldn't even listen to her plan although he'd already stripped off in front of them and slashed his arm to pieces for the sake of their stupid make-believe gang. She looked at Jackie helplessly. She sat smoking, watching, tutting, then let out an exasperated breath and stood up.

'Johnnie!'

In the corner he stood crying his eyes out, muttering to himself. He looked down at the floor to avoid her gaze. Jackie walked over and tried to put her hand on his shoulder but he pulled away. She persevered until he slowly let her touch him, put her arms around him, cuddle him. Suddenly his arms sprang to life around her back. He squeezed her tight.

'A dae love yi, Jackie. Honest A do. It's no right to hurt folk though.'

Stroking his hair, she shooshed him down.

'It's OK. Dinnae get so worked up. We dinnae want yi ti hurt anyone.'

'Ma airm hurts, Jackie. It's really nippin'.'

Jackie circled his back with her hand like she was winding a baby.

'It's awright, Johnnie. Jist dae this one thing an Al come back here an clean it up. Make it no sore.'

Letting go of her, he looked into her face.

'Really, yill come back wi' me again?'

'Aye, of course. Yill be in the gang thin, won't you?'

He smiled and sniffled and wiped his nose on his sleeve.

'Aye, OK, Am soarry. Al dae it. I didnae mean it.'

Jackie gestured to Johnnie. Claire walked over cautiously, worried that one wrong word might send him into hysterics again. He smiled at her, snorting, apologetic.

'OK, Johnnie. I don't want you to hurt her. Just scare her a wee bit. Me and Jackie have both done it already.'

'What?'

She told him the teacher lived in one of the stairs round the corner. Number 59. All he had to do was make a mess on her mat, just to annoy her. She deserved

it became of what she'd done to Jackie. They'd go with
him. Then they'd come back here and sort his tattoo.

'What sort of mess?'

'Oh, you know. A jobby. Just on her mat. We've both
done it. She's really horrible, Johnnie. You see, it's not
hurting her.'

He looked at Jackie for reassurance.

'Then yill come back here wi' me?'

'Aye Johnnie, A told you we would.'

'Promise?'

'Aye. Look, it's gettin' late. Yill hiv ti do it soon.'

He picked up his T-shirt, which was still attached to
his other clothes and pulled them on. They had to
describe the stair to him as he wouldn't be able to read
the number. Just round the corner, past the fish shop,
three stairs up. The blue door. He could run round
the block. They'd go through the back gardens and he
could let them in from the green. It would look funny
if the three of them went in the stair together.

As they repeated the instructions to him, he grinned,
getting into the adventure of it all again and sprinted
up the steps at the side of the canal, disappearing into
the fog. Giving him a minute's start so they wouldn't
be seen together, they ran up and through the park
themselves. They saw Johnnie running like his life
depended on it, at the far side next to the tennis courts
on to the street. Laughing at his new-found enthusiasm,
they jogged and chuckled across the grass.

The teacher's garden was accessed through someone's drive, over a wall and through a couple of fences.
Claire lived at the top of the street. Jackie and she had
seen the teacher in her garden one day when they'd
been stealing a T-shirt off a washing line.

Johnnie had already opened the door and was waiting for them in the garden when they got there. He was panting and excited like a big dog.

'OK, Johnnie. It's the last door on the top floor,' Claire whispered. 'We'll wait down here. Just shite on her mat then come and meet us.'

'How high is it? A dinnae like when it's high.'

The whites of his eyes glistened under the light from someone's window.

'It's no high. Yi dinnae need ti look down,' said Jackie, putting her hand on his shoulder to reassure him.

His neck was keening towards the entrance of the stair now. His tongue between his teeth again. He wanted to do it. He was ready. They pushed him gently along the passage and pointed up to the top landing.

'OK, just up there,' said Claire, barely audible, 'and remember what she's done to Jackie.'

'OK, OK,' he said, jumping quickly and quietly up the stairs two at a time.

'An dinnae make a noise,' whispered Jackie after him but he was already on the first landing.

'What's he like?' laughed Claire.

'Daft cunt!' said Jackie.

They walked into the centre of the stairwell and looked up. They could hear the soft smack of Johnnie's trainers on the steps. Finally he looked over the banister at the top and smiled, then looked a bit queasy and whined. Jackie gave him the thumbs up as his face disappeared back on to the landing.

They listened as hard as they could. There was a gentle ruffle of fabric. Jackie grabbed Claire's sleeve in disbelief and amusement.

'It's his troosers. Listen. He's taking them doon.'

They listened closely again and could hear him squeaking and straining, trying to soil the mat. Jackie touched Claire's arm then tiptoed towards the main door of the stair. Where was she going? Weren't they going to wait on him after all, thought Claire? Jackie stopped the door with her foot, leaned out and pulled the bell at the bottom. Claire heard it ringing on the top landing. Jackie came running back into the stairwell, laughing quite loudly now. Claire gazed upwards with her hand over her mouth to stop the laughter getting out. Johnnie was pushed against the rail of the banister, lying on the ground, wailing. She pointed upwards.

'What the fuck's he doin'?'

Both watched, bursting with amusement until the door opened. They didn't hear the teacher say anything but Johnnie started squealing and stumbling and bashing against the railing, trying to stand up. His bare bottom was pressed against the banister. He was trying to back away but he'd forgotten to pull his trousers up.

They suddenly there was a 'Whoop' sound and Johnnie was there, above them, flying downwards with his trousers around his ankles. It was like it was in slow motion. As they ran out the back door they heard a horrible, loud, crunching sound.

They vaulted over the wall, through the hole in the fence, through the drive and sprinted across the park, not stopping till they were back at the canal. They both stood wheezing at the bench, hands on their knees to hold themselves up. Unable to speak, Jackie shrugged across the canal.

Even when they got into the hut though and were breathing normally again, neither of them spoke. They just began cleaning up. Collecting the old tins and papers and wrappers in the box with the drawings and dumping them all in the canal. As they watched his belongings slowly suck down into the black water Jackie broke their silent lament with a flamboyant 'Whoop'. The same noise that Johnnie had made as he'd tumbled over the banister. His last noise.

Claire listened to her friend's renewed guffawing bouncing around inside the canal bridge. Her mind had gone completely blank so she wasn't even sure what was supposed to be so funny any more. But slowly she became infected by it and joined in. Laughing until her insides ached. Laughing because she was afraid not to. Laughing until she was sure she would never stop.

SNAPS

David McAlpine Cunningham

I look perennially distracted in snaps, as if I have just
spotted a herd of wildebeest sweeping towards the photographer, or the earth splitting open between his feet.
A blurred presence on the fringes, that's me, suffering
partial dismemberment from having an arm sacrificed
to the niceties of composition. What's more, no matter
how quizzically I contrive to meet the camera's unblink-
ing eye, I'm always usurped in the developed image by
my alter ego, the prowling loon. Examine any photo in
which I appear and you will be forgiven for assuming
that I am a mad second cousin, let out of the asylum
for the day but relegated to the sidelines so that the
male nurse to whom I am handcuffed won't stray into
shot.

Far too much faith is placed in snaps anyway. (It's a
good word that: Snap. It sounds like a trap shutting,
seizing and holding you at your least presentable.) They
will record who was where on which day. But they will
tell you nothing about how the participants actually felt.
Children are ordered to join hands that were moments
before fastened around one another's throats. In-laws
embrace who find the thought, let alone the presence
of one another detestable. Though I have striven to
evade capture, I have failed often enough for the barest

chronicle of my live to exist on film. Let's look at these photos together, you and I. It's amazing what they don't tell you . . .

I

PORTOBELLO, 1971, L–R: DAD, ME, MUM

The bonsai Christmas tree listing in the background tells you that I was born in late December. Its size and absence of decorations suggest that my parents could, at the time, scarcely afford a string of tinsel, let alone another mouth to feed. From this you might reasonable deduce that I was unplanned.

In the foreground, my father holds me like an unexploded bomb swathed in wool. His large, abrasive hands look like those of a manual worker. In fact, he is a golf pro. Then there's my mother. Long black hair, Cathy McGowan fringe, charcoal-lined eyes in the centre of a wan face. Her pained smile may be due to the rigour with which the surgeon sewed her up after my birth. Or it may be due to the fact that her husband responded to the news of his son's impending arrival by leaving early for the Swiss Open.

What snaps also don't tell you is who took them. This one could conceivably have been taken by either of my mother's parents – though her father was most likely in the bathroom at the time. (He spent most of his later life commuting between conveniences all over East Lothian.) So let's assume that it was my grandmother. Upon my father's defection to parts foreign, she moved in. Returning to find her installed in the one bedroom with her daughter and grandchild, he remained home just long enough to have clothes washed and his photo taken, then left again.

II
FALKIRK, 1974, L–R: MOIRA, DES, ME, JOYCE, FRASER, MUM, GRAN ETC.

In other words, my mother's sister, her husband, their daughter and son. The garden is that of my grand-parents' house. We are all standing on the gravel path that divides the lawn into two neat rectangles. Alliances and estrangements among family members are displayed by who occupies which rectangle on such occasions. Today we have all temporarily assembled on neutral territory to do our group impersonation of the happy clan. After the photo was taken, we no doubt dispersed again into our various coalitions.

Des, with his arm around Moira, who rests her head against his shoulder, worked on the oil rigs and was therefore something of an absentee, like my father. During periods of leave, he maintained his muscle tone by beating Moira up and bellowed at the children in a voice made powerful by competing with North Sea gales. Later, I recall, Moira sat with my mother on the left side of the garden and discussed their questionable taste in men. Both blamed lack of paternal affection. My grandfather sat on the other side with Des. He detested Des, but wished to demonstrate that any company was preferable to that of his own family. When my mother and I moved in after my parents' separation, he said nothing but registered his disapproval by even longer occupations of the bathroom.

III
FALKIRK, 1974, L–R: MUM, MOIRA

Indoors, the next day. Taken by me, which explains why the steps on which they are perched seem to be suffering from chronic subsidence. Looking at it, you might also be forgiven for wondering why Moira has a hand raised to shield her eyes, despite being out of the sun. In fact she asked Des for a divorce that morning and he responded by giving her a black eye. To conceal this, she improvised a spectacular fall downstairs. She and my mother now sit discussing their respective situations. You can tell from the looks on their faces that their trains of thought are running along parallel tracks.

IV
CHELTENHAM, 1978, L–R: GRAN, MUM, ME, RICHARD, JANICE, MOIRA, GLEN

Taken by Des, around his and Moira's dining-room table. My grandfather is dead, having finally failed to emerge from the bathroom one morning.

It's Christmas again, as the turkey stuffed to capacity in the centre of the table indicates. Moira, leaning over it, brandishes a carving knife. She does not look into the lens but below it, perhaps entertaining dangerous thoughts about the photographer's chest, or indeed other parts of his anatomy.

But who is Richard – watchful, tensely smiling Richard of the light tan, silver hair and raised glass? He is my stepfather-to-be, brought along by my mother for inspection by the rest of the family. In this snap he looks like the repository of much bonhomie, already well integrated. In fact he behaved towards Moira and my grandmother with distinct coolness, infuriating the former by brushing invisible crumbs off every seat before he planted his backside on it. He and my mother were married a few months later on a wild day when a salvo of sleet swept across the church like stinging confetti.

V

BEN CRUACHAN, 1984, L–R: RICHARD, MUM

On holiday, in fact their first attempt at a reconciliation. You can tell that some sort of unanimity has been achieved from the matching green anoraks they are wearing. In the background, a lurid evening sky is reflected in the waters of Loch Awe. A violent cross-wind plasters strands of my mother's hair across her face. She is snapped in the act of peeling them off and cramming them back under her hood. Richard stands beside her in his best Monarch of the Glen pose.

The rest of the holiday, conducted in an atmosphere of strained civility, was not a success. On the way home, he baited her, as he often did, with his near-suicidally reckless driving. Finally she exploded when he swung out behind a bus, only to be confronted with a heavy goods vehicle bearing down on us. He stopped the car to give the row his full attention. Sitting in the back seat, I turned up the volume of my personal stereo to smother their outpourings of resentment. As the flimsy plastic headphones vibrated to the sound of 'The Power of Love', I watched the windows turn opaque with their breath.

VI

VIAREGGIO, 1986, L–R: ME, LUIGI, GIOIA,
GIACOMO, DANIELLA

With my father's new son, new wife and her parents, crammed on to the sofa in the living room of the flat they all share. It's evening and our faces are freckled with orange light. This effect is achieved by the blind, which has recently been strafed with hailstones and now strains the sunlight like a colander. Photography is my father's new craze and we have been packed together like this for over thirty minutes while he waits for exactly the right shade of orange – not too red, not too yellow.

But our air of hunch-shouldered discomfort may have other explanations. Gioia was a waitress at a local club where my father taught golf between tournaments. He could speak little Italian; she little English. Marital conflict was, at first, confined to rudimentary arguments about ordering food and converting travellers' cheques. But, as time went on, they were able to learn more of one another's language and hence disagree about a wider range of issues with great fluency.

Discreetly removed from the still-expanding disaster area that was my mother's marriage to Richard, I didn't want to see it re-enacted Italian-style and mostly kept to myself throughout the summer, reading and cycling around the nearby farmland and into the mountains.

VII

OBAN, 1987, L–R: NIGEL, DOREEN, MUM,
SALLY, TOM, ME

Among new friends in the garden of another new home. I was recalled after five weeks in Italy. During my stay, I dreamed nightly of the tug-of-love battle that might ensue between my parents for possession of me. They stood an equal distance from me on either side. On the left, my mother tantalizingly rattled the keys of a gleaming new hatchback. On the right my father proffered a quantity of cash. I dithered between them, always waking before being required to make a choice. When I did return to Scotland (with a disappointing absence of fuss on either side), my mother and step-father announced a trial separation. Richard would stay in the family home and we would move into a Wimpey semi-villa which he had bought for that purpose.

So here we are. A barbecue is in progress, explaining the grey cloud that curls like gun smoke between our legs. Nigel and Doreen are our next-door neighbours. Nigel, rotund and bearded, brandishes a toasting fork, on the end of which is skewered an incinerated sausage. Sally is their daughter – short, slightly stocky, but daunt-ingly voluptuous and my girlfriend of one awkward month. Tom, being hoisted aloft by Sally, is her golden-haired younger brother, whose interests include per-secuting cats and breaking wind in public.

For once, the photo communicates a sense of jollity that is not entirely counterfeit. Meanwhile, in the house that was once again his own, Richard installed the woman he had been seeing for the previous three years. So we were all satisfied.

VIII

OBAN, 1989, L–R: RICHARD, ME

Dressed in black, side by side at my mother's funeral. Snapped by a spectacularly tactless, camera-fiend in-law. Alert as always, Richard has just placed a supportive arm around my shoulder. I flinch and thus look as if I have been caught in a spasm of grief. Behind us, the squat ranks of headstones march anonymously into the distance.

My mother discovered that she had cancer only a few weeks before the mandatory period of separation was over. Moving swiftly into action, Richard moved us back into the family home and installed his mistress in our vacant house, calculating that what he could save in alimony payments would cover her bills for the six months that my mother was given to live. Perhaps I am being unfair to him. I hope so.

IX
FORTE DEI MARMI, 1990, L–R: LUIGI, GIOIA

Further north, along the coast from Viareggio. They sit on one of the piles of tyres that fringe the go-kart track in the centre of town. Forte dei Marmi is a small enclave of prosperity in a farming region, but it makes this one, small concession to populism.

He sits on her lap and she tilts her head sideways to avoid being struck in the cheek by his flailing ice-cream cone. More and more often these days he improvises such a prank when a picture is about to be taken in order to banish her almost permanent air of solemnity. The state of her marriage to my father has altered. It used to be co-habitation punctuated by lengthy separation; now it is separation punctuated by briefer and briefer co-habitation.

I came to Italy with Richard's generous good wishes. When a discreet interval had elapsed, he recalled his mistress from her temporary exile with the intention of soon marrying her. I could hardly object. But, once again, I didn't want to see it happen. So I asked if I

could spend a 'year out' between school and some kind
of gainful employment with my father in Italy. I neglected to mention that my father was hardly ever in
Italy these days. Richard agreed, not without, I suspect,
a tinge of relief. The cheque which he pressed on me
to cover my expenses was so large that it really
amounted to a pay-off. I had the impression that I was
not expected to return.

Having sifted through this trove of images together,
you and I, let's bring the sequence to a temporary
conclusion . . .

X

PISA, 1990: ME

Taken by Gioia. She and Luigi remained with me until
my delayed flight was called. I spent a year looking after
him in the afternoons and dying of unexpressed love
for her in the evenings, I forced him to persist with his
hated English studies and he in return taught me a
good deal of demotic Italian. In the mornings I tried
to write first a precociously brilliant novel, then a precociously best-selling novel, then just any novel. I failed
at all three. My father reappeared now and then. Each
time he seemed surprised to see me, having been away
so long that he had forgotten I was staying with him.

Let's take a last look at me then. I am standing at
the entrance of the airport terminal, a sparse, cavernous
building in which all sounds seems to congregate at the
ceiling. Ironically, having been usurped by the prowling
loon in every other snap, here I look calm, assured
almost. True, my hair, cut the previous night by Gioia,
with contributions by Luigi, is long on top and shaved

at the sides, making me look like a *fascisto* in a bad wig. But there is an apparent reserve of calm in the eyes and a glow of prosperity about the tan. It is not the face of a young man about to leave his adopted family for an uncertain future in London with only a small suitcase and a neatly folded, uncashed cheque. It is not the face of a young man doomed never to declare an awesome crush on his Italian stepmother. It is not the face of a young man for whom a series of counterfeit images constitute the only evidence of his life so far. That's the problem with snaps. If they tell you anything, it's invariably a lie.

SIGNALS

G. A. Pickin

On a windswept day you can stand on the beach above Portpatrick and see Northern Ireland. Not just the slash of dark haze that passes for the Isle of Man when you're looking south, but a proper Irish profile, with its pointy nose in the air, as if giving a snub to Britain. But to make amends there's a chimney, one of those tall industrial ones, waving a slender handkerchief of smoke from its flue in a grand 'Halloo'. Looking at the map, I reckon this friendly gesture's from Carrickfergus, and I feel it would be churlish not to return the greeting.

We get quite a few of these panoramic days, and every one of them sees me standing on the beach, waving for all I'm worth when I know no one's about to see such daftness. It's daft for several reasons:

1. Although you can see quite a bit of detail, you couldn't possibly make out a figure, waving or otherwise,
2. The person I'm waving at has moved from the six counties to Malahide, so even if he *could* have seen me before he can't now, and
3. The person I'm waving at is a film star who doesn't even know I'm alive.

I say film star advisedly because although he's in lots of films (and on the stage with his own theatre company), even been nominated for an Oscar, he's hardly a household name.

Stephen Rea.

Go on, laugh. My husband did. Not even a tentative chuckle, but that sort of dismissive bark men have that means it's you, and not what you're saying, that they find so ridiculous.

Anyway, it wasn't as if I had the hots for Mr Rea. (Although . . . but no, I know it's foolish.) No, my daydream had me writing this screenplay for him, getting to know him, finding we enjoyed each other's company. Friendship, a meeting of minds.

The fantasy starts with me sending him this manuscript out of the blue. He almost chucks it when he realizes it's an unsolicited bit of writing. But instead he carries it to the breakfast table, and he and his wife Dolours decide to have a laugh over the cornflakes and read parts to each other. What they read there (naturally) intrigues them, and soon they find they're drawn into the story, into the characters, and that maybe, just maybe, there's something to this would-be screenwriter's work.

The story, as I imagine it, has depth and colour, and its subtleties would be brilliantly underplayed by Mr Rea. On impulse, he rings the telephone number listed on the cover sheet and arranges to meet me for lunch at Jasper's in the centre of Belfast.

I manage to sound cool on the phone, but upon gently replacing the receiver in its cradle, I leap about like a spring lamb (dressed at mutton), hugging the dog, and singing snatches of 'Wild Women Don't Get the Blues' as I rush out of the house.

Now in real life, I've got the girls to worry about. I get Marian next door to agree to collect them from school for me, then ring my husband to let him know I'll be out.

'Whyever do you want to go shopping in Belfast today?' he asks, annoyed. 'Why not wait till nearer Christmas? We'll go as a family, get all the presents bought.'

'I just need to get to a good bookshop,' I lied feebly.

'What about Ayr, or Dumfries? I could let you have the car tomorrow . . .'

'And I'd like to see the exhibition at the Ulster Museum,' (which isn't a lie, but that will have to wait). 'I'll be home by six if I catch the four o'clock SeaCat.'

That arranged, I go to Stranraer to buy the ticket. I always feel cold in Stranraer, although it's more sheltered than Portpatrick. The town clings tenaciously to the edge of Loch Ryan, the ferry terminals blocking the view of Ailsa Craig. When the tide's out you can see all the rubbish people throw overboard on their way across. If you lift your eyes past the headlands, Arran sometimes shows her broad back. But she never waves, she's too busy looking north to her sister islands. I can't say as I blame her.

Anyway, ticket in hand, I board the nearly empty SeaCat and find a place on one of the bench seats behind the captain, so I can watch Belfast approach. There's something solemn about the long line of shipyards that pass, the big Harland and Wolff signs overseeing a ponderous stillness as the 'Cat creeps into the quay. There's a courtesy bus that takes you straight into the centre, but I prefer to walk along the grimy Bangor ring road and up the narrow alleyways so that the centre, with its grand façades and wide avenues, looks all the more inviting. I go straight to Jasper's, where I find a corner table away from the toilets, and get a coffee to keep me going until he arrives.

Now I don't suppose Stephen Rea for one moment would ever dream of setting foot in Jasper's in real life. It's a quick and cheap cafeteria-style restaurant that does 'Ulster Fries All Day – 99p' as its chef's special. Egon Ronay doesn't come in to it. But even for the sake of maintaining my fantasy I can't afford to eat somewhere more realistic, so Jasper's it is.

When enough time has elapsed, I pretend to see him come in, go and introduce myself (very subtly, because to all the people *actually* in the café I have to seem normal or they'll have me sectioned), go through the queue once more and get myself a cottage pie and chips and a Coke. I sit down, and mentally click on my tape recorder, then face him with my biggest grin.

He's got his hair in those long lovely curls, and a stubbly beard that he's sported for the Field Day production of *Uncle Vanya*.

'I hope you're wanting me for the older man. I really enjoyed playing someone my own age for a change in *Uncle Vanya*.' Mr Rea looks pleased when I nod my agreement. 'Who have you got for the other parts?'

'Perhaps you know someone, an unknown wanting a break? Anyway, I wanted you first. Without you, the whole thing doesn't work.'

He gives me that sceptical/innocent look he's so good at from across the table, then smiles and reaches over to shake my hand.

'I think we may have a deal,' he says, and my adrenalin is doing so much overtime at the touch of his warm dry hand that I wonder he doesn't get an electric shock from my fingers. 'I'll give the script to Neil Jordan to read, and, if he'll agree to direct, we'll meet again and arrange a schedule.'

I can't believe he's saying this, that my shaky shaft shot into the air has fallen smack into the centre of the bull's-eye. I forget about being cool, grip his hand tightly with both of mine and gush: 'That's absolutely grand, Mr Rea. I'll die happy now, just knowing you've agreed in principle to doing it!'

I have forgotten that this is a fantasy, and people in the café are staring at me as I perform this strange gesture with my hands above my cottage pie and gabble inanely to the empty chair opposite. Fortunately, in Jasper's you pay before you sit down, so I just get up quietly and slip out the door, all eyes on me.

I spend the whole way back imagining phone calls to various businesses and arty individuals who might be willing to invest in the film. I lay it on thick to most of them, letting on without actually lying that Rea and Jordan are in the bag. By the time I've reached Stranraer, I have the promise of £4 million, which should be enough to draw the rest of the money I'll need.

'Did you enjoy the exhibition?' my husband asks as I waltz in the door, beaming. I almost make the mistake of asking 'What?' but a discreet cough and then a paraphrased rendition of a review I heard on the radio cover the gaffe. Or I hope they do, because he's looking at me in a most peculiar way, and I can feel my cheeks flushing with the lie, and the excitement, and the absurdity of it all.

The girls are full of stories about the dreaded James

(a boy in their class dubbed 'The Alien), and we all fall about giggling. We're still making each other grin at the dinner table by making finger antennae when my husband announces: 'I've applied for another job. In Leeds. The interview's next week.'

I'm still laughing, because somehow this seems as silly as the James scenario, but I can see by his face that he's in earnest, and I feel my chips and beans go glacial in the pit of my stomach.

'But you can't get Radio Scotland in Leeds!' I blurt out, and my husband's face goes stormy, then stony, and I know that no impassioned speech about a feeling of belonging and magic that my Portpatrick haunts instil in me will have any weight whatsoever against his need to move on, to move away from the stifling sodden blanket of a job he has to struggle with daily. If I love him, it's important now that I send the right signals. I want to support him, encourage him, to put my arms around him and let him know I love him. Instead, I say: 'I feel as if the bottom has just dropped out of my world.'

'Well, I've been crawling around at the bottom of mine for long enough, and I'm going for this job.' He glares at me, and his resentment shimmers off him in waves that distort the air around us. He pushes his half-finished meal across the table and strides out of the room, slamming the door behind him. I hear the front door bang as well, then the car engine catch third try. I close my eyes, releasing tears that clean two salty dots in the remains of the meal on my plate.

The girls carry on eating quietly, ignoring the waves and tears and momentous news, which will be stored wherever it is children put things that are too difficult to cope with at the moment. Beyond any wish or intention on anyone's part, they are becoming accustomed to these scenes.

Alone at the table, I switch on the fantasy.

'You don't have to apply for some stuffy administrator's job in Yorkshire. You can hand in your notice and start drawing, and sculpting, and making pots, and all the other things you haven't the time and energy left for after a day at work, because *I* am going to be earning good money at last.' And I go on to explain how Stephen Rea loved the script, and that the film was practically a foregone conclusion. He's pleased, naturally, and gives me a big hug.

'You dark horse, you,' he says, smiling and holding me out at arm's length as if to look at me properly for the first time. 'Why didn't you tell me you were working on a film script? I know you sell a few stories now and then, but a film? This calls for a celebration!' He twirls me round the room in delight, and we bundle the kids into their coats and, holding hands like teenagers, go down to the pub on the front and find a seat in the snug overlooking the harbour. We toast good riddance to my husband's job and a health to Messrs Rea and Jordan etc. and the success of my film.

I've been in bed reading for an hour when I hear him come back. I want to apologize and snuggle up to him, maybe have sex and make everything better between us, but instead I put the book down and pretend to be asleep when he comes in. He doesn't try to be particularly quiet, but he doesn't make any attempt to wake me properly either; he slips into bed and turns off the light without a word.

*   *   *

After seeing everyone off to work and school, I go through the essential minimum of work needed to keep the house within Health Inspectorate guidelines and sit down to do some rewriting. Neil has made some suggestions about one of the scenes, and I take time over it. It would be Stephen Rea's big moment, and it has to be right.

I send the revised script off, and Stephen rings the next week to arrange another meeting, this time in Stranraer (because I can't afford another trip to Belfast before Christmas in real life and anyway, I can't risk my husband's wrath by asking to go).

'You've done well,' he tells me over sandwiches in the Downshire Arms. 'The scene really feels right now. The motivation is there, there's room for me to play with body language as well as speech, and the dialogue is natural but telling. A brilliant bit of writing.'

I flush with pride. 'It's Neil's idea,' I say modestly, but he's having none of it. We talk about characterization and motivation in some of the later scenes. The feeling I get, talking through the creative process without fear of ridicule, is an enormous sense of achievement coupled with the exhilaration of a potentially limitless freedom.

I see Stephen off at the quay and catch the bus back to Portpatrick. Dinner is one of the least strained we've had in weeks, and my husband is trying to catch my eye all through the meal as I suddenly discover a million other places to look. It's over pudding that he tells us all what in my heart I knew was bound to happen.

'I got the job.' His face looks so animated and hopeful that I almost don't recognize him. The girls start to cheer and are already deciding how big a house we'll buy in Leeds and what the garden will contain. I smile and tell him how great it is, but we both know the impossibility of our situation. His triumph is my despair, just as this paradise for me is his nightmare. I will uproot myself and re-create a new version of me in Leeds.

'I'll put the house on the market first thing tomorrow,' I tell him, and his genuine pleasure at my ungrudging acceptance convects its warmth to the whole family. 'Then I think I'll nip over to Belfast for a last-minute bit of Christmas shopping. I know we were going to go together,' I say hastily, trying to clear his stormy brow like a high dry westerly breeze, 'but there are some things' – I wink at the children – 'I need to get on my own.'

He feels he can be magnanimous, and it's settled.

The next day, the house duly registered with the estate agents, I make the crossing and walk the glistening streets of central Belfast, the Christmas lighting reflecting off the rain-washed pavements in a futile attempt to brighten my spirits. Although this was meant to be my final meeting with Stephen before rehearsals start, I cannot bring myself to imagine the encounter. Instead I stride about, fighting back tears.

I get very wet standing by the steps of the Linen Hall Library, gazing across the road sightlessly, tears at last joining the rain on my face in a stupid, stupid show of grief over the loss of something I never had. When I pass by a post box on my way back to the ferry, I pull from my bag two envelopes, a heavy manila A4 one with a Belfast address, and a smaller, slim white one to be sent to Portpatrick. I force-feed them through the ungenerous mouth, and hear them land in the half-full belly.

Immediately, I want to call them back. One's too
foolish, the other too cruel, but I've no further fantasy
beyond madness to whisk me away from what I've done.

Stephen watched Dolours put the crumpled A4 envel-
ope on the sideboard, puzzled. The agent usually let
him know if there was a new script he might be interested in. Perhaps the agent had told him and he'd
forgotten, what with rehearsals, and the move so immi-
nent. Either way, it could wait now, until he got to
Malahide.

Today was their last day here, and Stephen wanted
to say goodbye to places. At each stop he paused, taking
in slow deep breaths as if the air of each soon-to-be
abandoned haunt could fill him with longing and regret
as it filled his lungs. But the emotions stubbornly
refused to come, the brutal or poignant past of each
spot remaining cold and distant, like text in a history
book.

Frustration drove him further and further from the
city, until he stopped at last at the old chimney at Carrickfergus. He climbed half-way up the hill behind the
slender red column and sat down on a cold stone,
watching the frail plume of smoke snake lazily upwards
into a faultless blue sky. Some movement drew his gaze
out on to the water and across to Scotland. He stood
slowly and shaded his eyes against the low winter sun,
scanning the coast for some sign of the motion's origin.

There it was again, a wide regular sweep from side
to side.

He mounted the steep slope to the very top of the
hill and turned. It was still there, the vague notion of
a wave, no more than a play of light upon the sea, no

doubt. Without really understanding it himself, he lifted his arm and began to wave back, a little hesitant movement at first, and then the great, double-armed signal of a once-desperate man who knows somehow, after many false hopes, that this time he is about to be rescued.

MANOEUVRES

Lizbeth Gowans

It was egg week again. Ella Yuill stood with her mother in the kitchen wiping clean two pails of fresh-laid eggs, their farm's fortnightly contribution to the war effort. Tomorrow someone would collect them for the packing station. Ella gently rubbed a dirty place and smiled at something.

'D'you mind the time I asked about shells? When I was wee? When I used to think our fighting men chucked *eggs* at the enemy?'

Her mother paid scant attention. 'Hm. What aboot it?'

'Well, I ken what war shells look like, from the *Adventure* pictures, but I *still* think of eggs, only huge. It must be those splat bits they draw – like this.' She laid down her egg to draw in the air the explosion figure she meant, but her mother was paying no attention at all now, gone back to the thoughts behind her sad-angry look.

Certainly, the news didn't seem good. Though her parents sat glued to the wireless a lot and listened to bulletins together, they never talked about the war in between times. They just had these awful expressions, the very same as if they'd quarrelled, had their own wee war at home.

Someone passed the window and a familiar voice

shouted in at the back door, 'Post!' Ella ran to get the *Daily Express* from him, eager for the next two Rupert pictures and the bit story. Later, she would crayon them, cut them out, and paste them into an old Black's catalogue. Three days' worth of Rupert nicely fitted a page, Nutwood covering the world of tackety boots, oilskins and sou'westers.

'Here's your paper, *a'ghraidh*. And gif your daddy this. Fery, fery important, this. Chust a minute.' He drew back the postcard he was about to hand over. 'Is your mother in?'

Her mother came to the door, egg in hand. 'Aye, Fearghas. What is it?'

He handed her the card. 'Now, see that your man kets this. It's an adfance notice from the Ministry. I suppose they'll pe sending them periodically.'

Her mother read the card, both sides, and looked at the postman. 'This is for the morn. Damn short advance notice, is what my man'll say. An' he'll be right.'

'As long as he kets it.'

'What if you'd not been able to get up the road, eh? What if there'd been a blizzard?' She was getting roused, waving the card at the Postie, who was staring back at her in dismay.

'Well,' he finally said, 'if you think apout it, it's not likely they'd pe out on manoofers in a plizzard, now is it?'

But she wasn't pacified. 'Why no? I'm shair the fightin' across yonder doesny stop for blizzards. Nae doot the sodjers hae tae learn in a' conditions. Onywey ye look at it, this is short notice.'

'Aye, well, I'm chust the post, Mistress Yuill. You'll haf to be taking it up with the Ministry.'

'Aye. I see that. Nae offense tae you, Fearghas. Will ye have your tea as usual?' He would. Ella breathed clear, and went to see what new predicament Rupert was faced with. Talk about manoeuvres. That man who did Rupert was a dab hand at them, keeping the problems of Nutwood far from the really dangerous or frightening and guaranteeing that somehow rescue was always out there for the wee bear, no matter what dark cave he got thrown into. They were baby stories, she knew that, but she told herself they were for Jean when she'd be old enough to read them and not have to wait for the paper to see what the next manoeuvre would be. It was a great word, *manoeuvre*. She whispered it, saying it like Fearghas. *Manoofer*. Then *manooferpoard*, and laughed to herself.

The postcard was propped against the clock-face on the mantelpiece. Her father always looked at the clock when he came in or listened to the news, drawing his watch from his waistcoat pocket to tally the times. It was the best place for the card.

Next morning, as she set off down the fields with Davy and Watty to school, Ella was gratified to see their father taking Jean for a toddle along the beech path behind the farm. It was a rare sight, for he was usually off to the hill early before any of them woke up and was too tired to do more than sit by the wireless in his chair when he came back. These periodic cards from the Ministry might be no bad thing, she thought. Maybe some days away from the hill would improve his moods. Certainly he looked easy and kind with Jean this morning, at peace with himself. But she knew it was just a matter of waiting for the next time he wasn't.

She remembered something Fearghas had once said

to her mother on the doorstep. 'Pe crateful your man is eksempt, Mistress Yuill. Enough poor laddies are coing off to the war, and may the chust Lord cause some cood to come of it all. He mofes in mysterious ways, you know.'

His somethings to perform, Ella finished tacitly, vaguely knowing the rest from somewhere.

She remembered, too, her mother's reply. '*I'm* grateful. But Andra's no. No him. He takes it ill that they wouldny have him. Tellt him tae gaun hame an' dae his bit on the ferm, for that's where he was needit the maist. But he didny believe them. He came hame an' tellt me they were a' liars, that the truth was they didny think he was guid enough tae fecht for his country like the rest o' the men his age. An' ever since, Fearghas, I'm tellin' ye, he's no fit tae live wi'.'

'What for does he haf to be fechtin'?' Fearghas had asked. 'Forpy, he'll pe with the home cuard, will he no?'

Her mother had given a puff of laughter. 'What? The home guard? You should jist hear him on the home guard. He only went the yin time. Said it was a pure make-a-fool-o', because when it came tae the drills an' they hadny enough rifles, guess whae got yin o' the byre brushes instead? Oh no, he said, if he was tae wield a byre brush he'd dae it at hame where sic things had their proper place an' dignity. Oh, but he was black-burnin' affrontit, an' he never went back. He hasny gotten ower the shame o't. He feels it sair.'

And, Ella added in her mind, he takes his terrible discontent out on the rest of us, especially Mum, who can't do or say anything right these days.

On the way home from school, she scanned the dark line of the hill ridges behind the brae where the farm stood, looking for flashes or explosion splats in the sky, but there was nothing to see. Yet she could hear a muffled rumbling from time to time from that direction.

Strange voices and laughing from the kitchen slowed her down at the threshhold, wondering. Then thudding feet behind her made her turn. Two soldiers in khaki came round the corner of the steading. One of them bent over on one leg to pull up his socks, like a laddie in the playground, and she saw he was wearing sand shoes, like them at school who couldn't afford good shoes. They looked at her kindly.

Then a voice from the door said, 'In here, lads.' Dressed the same, he waved them in then said to her, 'Aye, hen. That you hame fae the school?'

There seemed to be a whole regiment of them in the kitchen, sitting round the table, on the fender box, on the wide window sill. Her mother was pouring tea into all the cups in the house ranged on the table and there were big plates of scones and pancakes out, with fresh butter and blackcurrant jam. Her mother's face was glowing with the pleasure she always felt feeding her baking to a crowd that was all eyes for it.

'Right. There's milk and syrup for the tea, and ye just help yoursels now,' she said. 'If you're tellin' us the truth that naebody's gaun tae be lookin' for ye, then you're welcome to partake.'

One of the older soldiers laughed. 'Listen, this is a' part an' parcel o' the manoeuvres, findin' a place o' safety. Mind you, I'd maybe desert for a taste o' this grub, efter a' that bully beef they've been feedin' us.

Right, boys?' Hearty agreement was expressed round the gathering.

In the press of company, Ella hadn't noticed her father right away. He was in his chair by the wireless as usual, smoking, listening to the crack with a look that she couldn't place. Whenever folk came round the steading, they'd be asked in, the kettle put on. It was the way. The soldiers must definitely have been asked in. Maybe it was because there were so many of them that her father had that lips-parted look, as if he'd come on the burn in flood and was hunting for a way across.

Then she saw a more familiar look take over, aimed at her mother for enjoying all this too much, being the centre, when look at him, taking a back seat. *Oh no*, Ella thought, making her way round the edge of the crowd to go up the stair and away out of sight, *she'll catch it when everybody's left. I know that look. Why did he ask them in anyway, if it's going to make him look like that? Why are folk so stupid?*

She meant to stay up the stair a while, but she was starving and soon crept back down to see if any of the baking was still going. On the bottom stair she stopped. It was all quiet in the kitchen, except for the sound of her father telling something. She sat down and listened. It was the story she'd heard told several times to various folk, like uncles from the town, when they got to talking about the war and the great air battle over Britain.

'Ye've never seen anything like *this*,' he was saying. 'I'll never forget it. I was oot lookin' my sheep on a hill abin the Whiteadder, doon Abbey-St-Bathans wey, in the Borders, an' here I heard this plane comin'. It soondit awfy close, but I couldny see tae begin wi' where

47

it was comin' fae. So I stood still an' listened, an' then I seen it. It was followin' the coorse o' the river, jist abin the trees. Ye could see the leaves bendin' under it. The engine was jist aboot giein' oot. What a mess! The wings, the fusillidge, riddlt wi' bullets. Aye. Fair riddlt. But he was heidin' hame, ye see, an' determined tae dae it. I dinny ken hoo he wis managin' tae keep it in the air, but he did. I watched him bring it richt up the water an' oot o' sicht. I dinny ken where he was makin' for, but we never heard o' a plane gaun doon in thae pairts, so he must've gotten hame a' richt. An' ye ken, a' the time I wis watchin' him, I was wishin' I could've done somethin' tae help the laddie, the pilot, like. Cheer him oan, if nothin' else. I mind I said, oot lood, *gaun yersel, son, that's a boy*. But I wis jist a shipherd on a hill, no daein' much at a', eh? Nothin' much tae test the sort o' hert *I* had, eh? No like yon pilot. No like you boys, eh?'

From the soldiers there was a surge of sound, a kind of half-laughing that asks someone who they think they're kidding. 'Listen, man,' said a voice, 'we couldny conduct a war athoot men like you. Ye ken that yersel. Look at the day. This gies us mair hert tae gaun back tae the job than a' yer grand speeches tae the troops. Believe you me. Am I no right, boys?'

Behind the door, Ella wondered if her father believed them. Did *she* believe them? How could a pile of pan-cakes – even her mother's spanking ones – match one of Churchill's speeches? It sounded like a mere thing to say, to tell a man running himself down overmuch, especially one at whose table you were stuffing yourself. And yet . . . wasn't this what was meant by keeping the home fires burning? Why couldn't her father see the usefulness of all that, and him part of it? Why did he hanker after something else?

You'd almost think he'd been reading too many *Adventure* stories with their pictures of daring exploits in the skies, on the high seas, behind a machine-gun on a rocky hill. But he only read the *Express* where the pictures were pretty tame compared to the *Adventure* drawings.

The soldiers went, full of thanks, leaving several tins of Spam on the table as barter for the baking. They said they'd pass on to the next lot word about the grand sanctuary they'd found in the war zone. Like being, one said, mentioned in dispatches – unofficial, of course.

Her mother began to redd up the table, a smile on her lips that died at the look being cast across at her from the chair by the wireless. Ella's heart thudded, angry that the kind, easy person he was that morning with Jean hadn't stayed long and that Jean herself, playing there on the rug with her doll, was somehow, so far, exempt from knowing this.

'Ella?' Her mother's voice was strained. 'Go an' bring in the cows for me. Take Jean wi' ye. Thae sodjers have kept me back. On ye go.'

Part of her was grateful for this while another continued to hum with trepidation. Hurrying to the cows' field, she could still hear the noise like far thunder over the hills.

Twice more, while eluding the enemy on the hill, batches of soldiers found their way to the Yuills' kitchen, were fortified and left Spam which the bairns liked for its smooth, salty taste and jelly round the edges. Every time, though he chaffed with the soldiers a good deal, Ella noted that her father was watchful in a queer way, waiting, she was sure, for one of them to say something nice to her mother, about her baking even, so that he could tuck it away and bring it out later and blame her. Why, she asked herself a hundred times, is he not glad that folk like her? She can't help it, being a fine baker and being so . . . well, bonnie to look at, her with her black shiny hair and eyes browny-green, like rushes.

The time one of the soldiers produced a new, flowered pinny from his back pocket and gave it to her mother along with the Spam, saying, 'It'll go wi' your e'en,' Ella's stomach somersaulted. Her eyes flew to her father's face and, sure enough, there was the look. Only, now, in that churning moment, she knew it for the look of someone watching a person who can do what he cannot, and he takes it ill.

That night, in the dark, Ella woke to a sense of some commotion and distress, then the sound of feet flying down the stairs. She listened for other feet following, but none came. She crept softly down to the kitchen. There in her nightgown by the window, both hands braced on the sill, head bowed, her mother was muttering passionate words, only half audible. '*I wish . . . wis deid. I wish . . . wis deid.*'

Ella froze. Wish what? Who? What was that she said? She came over and touched her mother's arm, afraid to ask anything, afraid if she said a word she would start with that crying that cracked your chest and made you wish to die, just the way her mother was saying she did.

'Oh Ella, Ella. My lamb. Your mother's jist a wee bit worn oot. Come on, I'll cuddle in wi' you an' Jean.'

A few days later, Ella passed Fearghas on his way with the post. 'Have you a postcard the day, Fearghas?'

'Aye, *a'ghraidh*, among other bits.'

So, she thought, more trials. If only the soldiers wouldn't come any more. If only her father could have his wish and be a soldier too. If only they didn't live here.

That same afternoon, homeward bound, she heard the guns. They were clear and loud, unmistakable. So her mother's early complaint about the postcards had been right, for this was surely the shortest notice yet. In fact, when she got home, it proved to be no notice at all, for there was no card propped in front of the clock and her mother was beside herself with anxiety.

'Did you no get the card?' Ella asked, fearful.

'No! Nae warnin' at a'. This is a punishment! God's punishment!'

'But . . .' Ella went to the bundle of post still on the table and spread out the envelopes. The *Scottish Farmer* was there, two catalogues, three brown envelopes, the *Express*. No card. Where was it? Mystified, a terrible thought came to her on an echo of her mother's desperate wish in the dark that night which she'd not been able to forget. Had it been *I wish he wis deid*? Had there been another of their rows this morning, making her that desperate again, only worse?

But her mother was truly wild with worry, so that couldn't be. Was it just a terrible wish coming true to punish her mother for wishing it? God's punishment, she'd said. Who was he punishing? How could Fearghas have made such a mistake?

Frantic, Ella struck at the stupid brown envelopes on the table and swept everything to the floor. Jean toddled over to pick the mess up and, as she lifted the heavy *Scottish Farmer* by its edge with both hands, she shook it up and down the way she always did when she'd managed a tricky lift, and out of the hanging pages slid the familiar card.

In awe, Ella bent for it, seeing the great cleverness of the way the punishment was happening.

They watched and listened for hours at the door, and when Jean and the boys were put to bed, Ella and her mother waited on into the deep dusk.

And, in time, at last, first the trembling dogs arrived in the steading, and then, staggering and half crawling home to his wife and children, came the shepherd, Andra Yuill, as subsequent, entirely unofficial dispatches described it, commending his bravery in getting himself out of the war zone, despite being struck in the neck by a piece of flying shell and being badly concussed.

Like many victims of battle stress, he was never quite the same again, as his heart had taken a severe strain, and he was medically advised to leave that rugged hirsel in the Grampians and take on an easier place, with field flocks. By the time he had recovered enough to do that, the war was finished and manoeuvres were over.

Shortly before the lorry was to take them out of the Grampians, Ella Yuill ran up to the hill gate for a last look at the dark heather ridge, behind which the unseen growling peril had lurked, moving according to plan, practising for a much bigger one to come, and that thing that Fearghas had once said about the just Lord came complete into her mind, and in his voice. *He mofes in mysterious ways His plunders to perform.*

A SLAP IN THE FACE

Jonathan Falla

In her grandeur as Professor of Gynaecology, Leila had her own office at the Khartoum School of Medicine. Among the monolithic foreign texts, her juniors were often amused to see a colour book of school geography. They had no idea why it was there. The Professor was an enigma, formidably skilled but unmarried, with few close friends and a ferocious reputation. Colleagues admired – and went in awe of her.

Had they dared ask, she would have told them that the book came from her father's house. It was his own, from his schooldays.

Leila had first tugged it from the shelf when she was just five years old. Inside, the little girl found a speckly picture of a white mass crashing into water of a peculiarly intense azure. The colour was crude and the illustration bewildered Leila. Every day she saw the Nile at Omdurman, but this looked nothing like it. The Nile's banks were low and dun and did not fall, did not swamp the little skiffs or barges or menace them at all. In the photograph, there was a sleek red boat (quite unlike the oily Nile ferries), and this boat must be huge for there were ant-like figures gathered on the deck, and the blue-white wall was mightily tall above it, and it was teetering and toppling!

53

'That is a glacier,' her father had said, leaning over the child perched on the black ottoman, 'made all of ice such as we have in our kitchen. That is a ship, and this is the Antarctic Ocean which is a water wider than the desert but utterly cold, Leila.'

This, at five, was the limit of Leila's notion of the world beyond Sudan. Later, she took an ice cube from the kitchen and, with it in her mouth making her palate ache, she sat with the book on her lap gazing at the picture: a blue desert on to which the frigid mountains fell.

Mahmoud al-Haq was completely delighted with his daughter's curiosity. Not long after, he came home from work carrying a battered cardboard box and called to the whole house that he had a gift for his girls. The box was heavy; Leila and Khamisa shuffled in silent speculation. Mahmoud placed the load on the dining table and they closed in on it.

'Wait!' he commanded, and went again to the car. He returned with a second box.

'Now you may open one box each,' he said.

Khamisa, older and stronger, heaved out a large volume bound in green plastic. She put it down at once, peering into Leila's box to see what else there was. Both cartons were filled with books: sixteen of them, all the same.

'What is this?' the girls' mother wanted to know. Enormously pleased with himself, her husband stood the books up between the two boxes.

It was an encyclopaedia, second-hand. Mrs al-Haq picked up *Quebec–Steel* at random. Inside the front cover was a stamp which (had she been able to read) would have told her: UNITED STATES INFORMATION

SERVICE LIBRARY – WITHDRAWN. Although the books showed only modest signs of wear, the edition was some thirty years old.

'So what is the use of it?' demanded Mrs al-Haq. Her husband, predicting this complaint, had already prepared a defence.

'Our nation,' he parried glibly, 'is, at the very least, a century behind the latest developments in America. A few years' leeway will not be a great handicap.'

'I do not understand what you are saying,' said Mrs al-Haq. 'I merely wish to know what you think our girls will be doing with such books? They know no English, they have yet to read Arabic.'

Khamisa (just started at school) slipped away from the table and switched on the television. Leila continued to turn the pages, dazzled by a thousand pictures of things whose name and nature she could hardly guess at. Her father beamed indulgently at his daughters.

'You shall see,' he purred, 'you shall see. This shall be a tool for their futures!'

'I hope they do not waste their futures as readily as you waste our money,' said his wife, heading for the kitchen to berate the servant for indolence. Hours ago, she'd ordered *halawa*, boiled lime and sugar for the stripping of bodily hair.

Corporeally and metaphorically, Mahmoud towered above his daughters. At least, that was his idea. He thought of himself as a lighthouse, tall and stern and bright. But he indulged Leila and Khamisa endlessly, playing, chattering, reading with them while other Omdurman fathers smoked away their evenings in cafés. Mahmoud's girls knew themselves to be the centre of his world.

Mahmoud al-Haq (so he told everyone at the National Bank) was an ardent and humane progressive. When she was older, this puzzled Leila. She knew that the vast majority of her opinions were inherited whole-sale from him: she had been born with liberal notions in her blood. Indeed, when she examined the broad spectrum of her convictions, she knew that the more reasoned an opinion seemed, the more certainly she had taken it on trust from her father.

So how (she asked herself) had her father come by his own views – given that *his* father had been a minor tribal chief of the most crusty conservatism?

Once, when they were small, Mahmoud took his girls to see the Omdurman camel market. His tribe was the Bani Amer; he intended Khamisa and Leila to taste that particular glory and to compare the wild Kababish of Kordofan and the lineages of the north. But he had forgotten the drought, the famines, the grasslands' decay into utter desert. When they came to the market field, there was a dreary pall of yellow dust from the hooves of an astonishing throng, hundreds upon hundreds of camels. There were huge stud bulls and light racing camels, brood mares and their young, all the treasure and pride of the tribes. And all were up for sale. The nobility of the sands were destitute and were asking a pittance for their entire herds. But the animals were ragged and diseased, staggering hulks of bone and mange. No one was buying.

Profoundly shocked, Mahmoud held his daughters by the hand and stared at the rout of tradition. Leila felt his grip tighten uncomfortably on her own. Anxious, she looked up at him and saw his gaze turn to the road nearby where the trucks and cars flocked, every one of them Japanese.

'We can do nothing here,' he said in a whisper.

Then there was the day when the girls and their mother were sunk into the black leatherette settee in front of the television watching an Egyptian soap opera. Mahmoud in passing had scornfully told them to switch to a Sudanese series – only to be told that there was no such thing.

And there was the day he came home from work incandescent with humiliated anger, having discovered that every one of the foreign banks in Khartoum could transfer money out of the country within twenty-four hours, whereas the antique systems of the National Bank could not move funds between two departments in much less than a week.

He winced and shrank at these experiences, again and again. His conviction and determination grew that the family al-Haq would put their best efforts into redressing the country's shame.

Though he yearned for a son, Mahmoud al-Haq never blamed his wife, nor would he divorce her as his friends advised. He declared that his girls were as good as anybody's boy; several of his acquaintance privately thought this claim offensive. Mahmoud called his daughters the vanguard of a new Sudan. He would not hear of having them circumcised, and it was axiomatic in the house that the children would proceed to university and thence to professional responsibilities.

So he would linger with Khamisa and Leila, enthusiasm writ broad upon his face like some 'artist's impression' of a model father in his modern house with his go-ahead little girls.

'What will you be, Khamisa?' he said, having gathered them on the sweaty black settee with the elderly encyclopaedia's pictures of the Seven Wonders of the Ancient World. A crude air-cooler, Khartoum-made, dripped on to the terrazzo floor. The machine was stuffed with watered straw and sat on a trestle in the yard outside, roaring through a hole in the wall. 'A doctor? Leila, shall your sister be a doctor?'

Khamisa was frowning at a pen rendition of Babylon's Hanging Gardens. Leila was in awe of her prim big sister who, even at primary school, their father intended for the Sciences. Khamisa ruffled the pages, pausing at a red-and-black cross-section of the heart. Mahmoud crowed.

'You see? You see this?' he shrilled to his wife as she laid his coffee tray on the glass table. 'Look what she picks out! The heart, look, instinctively she goes for that! She will be the foremost heart surgeon in Sudan!'

Their mother gave a sour little smile. She had some thoughts on surgery herself. Leila was five, Khamisa seven.

Mahmoud turned on through the volumes, and found that colour diagrams accompanying the article on reproduction had been excised. But, of course, the encyclopaedia was second-hand and from a library. Anyone could have done it. He cursed vehemently the narrowness of Sudanese minds and Khartoum education. He repeated these thoughts rather loudly at the Bank and in the fragrant cafés of the souk. Some of his friends wished he would learn a little moderation.

*   *   *

That Friday morning – their father was at the mosque – Leila found her mother putting Khamisa into the prettiest of new clothes. She was hurrying, tugging roughly at the zips and ties, while Khamisa stood curiously pale and quiet, clinging to a new bangle in pink metallic plastic. Leila watched from the doorway, scratching her right ankle with her left big toe.

'Why is Khamisa having new things?' she murmured, unhappy at her sister's expression. She was jealous of that full red dress embroidered with little black camels about its hem, but felt no desire to wear it just now. Her mother, sewing on a hook, was flustered and did not look up.

'Another day for you, my precious,' she said to Leila. Then, taking on her arm a yellow plastic basket in which fresh underclothes of Khamisa's lay folded, she led the two girls out into the sandy street to a house ten minutes' walk away.

For much of that morning, Leila crept from corner to corner contriving to be forgotten. There were four of Khamisa's schoolfriends, a crowd of women and a reek of cloying perfumes that made Leila want to gag. There was singing that had nothing to do with joy, everything to do with blotting out cries. There was a feast spread out, *marara* of raw chopped liver with onion, lime and blistering pepper – but Leila felt no hunger, only a nausea of apprehension.

The little girls were given fizzy drinks and coconut sweets and were seated on a couch in their new dresses, but Leila did not see them smile. The women fussed about them and shrilled, 'This is your wonderful day!' but Leila saw blind terror in her sister's face. Khamisa clung to the blue glass of juice but did not sip, did

59

not move. She was petrified; she would speak to no one.

There was a back room to which the children were led one by one with shouts: '*Bring the little bride!*' When Khamisa was taken, Leila slipped away to the kitchen porch and looked in through the grimy louvres. She saw her sister stretched out on a rush mat like a newly slaughtered animal about to be paunched. The flock of women knelt about Khamisa grasping her wrists and heaving her skinny legs apart. The pretty red dress with palm trees was hauled up round her waist, her panties discarded. Leila saw her sister's torso squirm and twist in protest. She saw a lady in dark green robes crouch between the convulsing legs. Then the knees were suddenly rigid, there was blood and Khamisa screaming, and someone led Leila away from the window.

Mahmoud's rage knew no bounds – but the thing was done. For all his cursing and threats, for all he slapped his wife's face terribly, he could not replace the flesh sliced off his daughter. He shouted that he would send the culprit to jail – but no one would give him a name. Khamisa spent two weeks in the back room with her legs bound together, the wounds closed with cigarette papers. Her pudenda were smothered in egg-white that became crisp and flaky, and was stained and streaked dark red. She took a high fever and the doctor came to inject her, muttering darkly about unsterile procedures. The girl lay mute, her hair clung in black sweaty snakes to her cheek and neck and a sour reek that Leila never forgot came from the room.

One evening, Leila heard her father speak words to her mother that were clear and simple and yet she could not understand. He said, 'Do that to my Leila, and I shall kill you.'

What could he possible mean? Leila appreciated that one killed chickens before eating them, but could not readily apply this idea to her mother. If her mother understood, there was no audible reply. For several days Mrs al-Haq went about tight-lipped, smiling down at the floor like a woman who knows that she has done her duty in the face of dull ignorance.

Mahmoud redoubled his educational efforts. He took the girls to every part of the Three Towns at the meeting of the two Niles. He showed them the palace steps where Kitchener in a white dress uniform fell with a spear through his ribs; they saw the swirling dance of the *darawish* in the shadow of the silver dome of the Mahdi's tomb; they witnessed the strut and swagger of all-comers Nubian wrestling on the dirt in front of the Khalifa's house.

He also purchased more books – some of them new – to an extent that Mrs al-Haq wept and pleaded with him to remember his paltry salary. He took Leila and Khamisa to the museums and the university, to the zoo where sad gazelles nosed at limp fodder and there was a dead fox in a neglected corner that made Leila sick and her father shout at a keeper: '*For shame!*' They went on the greasy black ferry to the groves of Tuti Island, and to the dusty botanical gardens. They went down-river on the steamer to inspect the vast cotton scheme of the Gezira.

Mahmoud declared they'd make a family picnic of this and his wife complied, bringing *kisra* bread of fermented millet, thin and sour, with stews of mutton and okra, oiled beans, omelettes and halva. They ate under a tree on the riverbank – after which Mahmoud with a resolute expression led the girls to clamber on to a concrete sluice among the grand irrigation works.

'What can he be thinking of?' their mother yawned. Mahmoud remained there with his girls in obedient silence beside him, Leila puzzled and watchful, Khamisa bored. He gestured to left and right, indicating the docile water that flowed in its channels and the cotton plants in regiments. Perhaps he was hoping that Khamisa (who'd been a little cool about medicine) might take inspiration here and become a leading agronomist one day. Perhaps Leila might study hydrology. In some important arena, surely, his daughters would be powerful and effectual as he had never been, never *would* be in his fatuous bank labours.

He spoke later (though it never came about) of a trip by car to Port Sudan, to view the Red Sea: 'It is neither Red nor Blue, Leila, but it is something for you to witness!' Bizarrely, he proposed taking them to the railyards where the broken locomotives stood. For once, Khamisa exchanged her sullen boredom for open rebellion. She'd become headstrong, taut with teenage willpower, and used cruel words. She told her father that he was weird, that inspecting irrigation technology was dull but at least comprehensible, whereas inspecting *broken* railway engines was eccentric, was perverse, was *laughable*! She hinted that all Khartoum said so – and Mahmoud lost his nerve and did not insist.

'It is up to you, absolutely,' he declared. 'My girls have their futures in their own hands. This is, of course, the most important lesson.'

But Leila went with him uncomplaining, and it

became accepted that these curious tours were for Mahmoud and Leila only. Leila never quite knew, even when the visits continued into her own teens, what she was supposed to think of her country. Perhaps his point was this: that she *could* be (if she so wished), she *might* be (there was nothing that should stop her; he'd see to it!) that very chief technician who would start her nation's trains again. Mahmoud would stand beside his girl, staring despondently at some spectacle of backwardness with his hand rising a little from his side as though he dearly desired to enthuse, to speak proudly, but felt his wrist weighed down with the decay of everything.

'Look,' her father said, wherever they were, said over and again, '*Look!*' as though just in the looking she would find the vocation to be everything necessary, everything so glaringly needful in Sudan.

These trips continued year by year until Leila was twelve. Though he could by no means forget the mutilation of his firstborn, perhaps Mahmoud now thought Leila safe.

They went away, mother and daughters, on a holiday. They went to Sennar, two hundred miles in a bus southward between the Blue Nile and the railway that was not working. They went for three weeks to stay with an aunt, while Mahmoud al-Haq attended his office. There he sat doggedly, day after day, penning unread summaries of last year's reports for purposes he never understood. Around him, clerks in neat khaki uniforms and old leather slippers totted columns on sheets of cheap grey foolscap, while lady secretaries in blue and amber chiffon robes pressed the keys of massive typewriters that clacked so *slowly*, lashing into the carbons like a military policeman's whip. Cowed messenger women, silent and creeping, brought coffee and memos to the Chiefs of Department who would look at them next week. There were three printer-calculators in the room, but only one functioned. The standard fan juddered, oscillating jerkily, like an awkward question that always came back to him. Mahmoud could think of no answer other than patience.

Of an evening, while his women were away, he went to the souk cafés and listened to the talk. He needed company, of course, and these were decent men. But in his heart he knew that they had little to say to the future. That was reserved for his daughters.

The bus brought the family back and Mahmoud embraced the girls fondly. Khamisa shuffled into the lounge and lay on the black settee complaining of a headache from the bus. Leila was very quiet and still. When Mahmoud kissed her on the cheek, she leaned towards him almost imperceptibly. Puzzled, Mahmoud watched her walk slowly towards the bedroom. She looked pale and moved stiffly, as though all her joints were inflamed. Her mother watched Leila also, then observed tartly that they'd been on a bus all day so he wasn't going to expect song and dance, was he?

Khamisa returned to school the next day, but Leila did not get up at all. Her mother dismissed enquiries, saying that she was just a teenager and they were all the same: let her rest, please, and don't fuss. But when Mahmoud came home in the afternoon, he found Leila with her face buried in the pillow and the pillow soaked with sweat.

'What is wrong with her?' he demanded of his wife. 'Have you called the doctor?'

His wife mumbled something and sidled out of the bedroom. Surprised, Mahmoud pursued her.

'Have you called the doctor? And why not? Leila is unwell, can't you see?'

Still the girl's mother mumbled.

Mahmoud bellowed at her: 'Send that servant girl at once. Heavens, what is it with you, woman? If you are not talking today, I shall send her myself. Our girl is sick, let us have some action in this house!'

The physician came, a personal friend. Mahmoud, fearing malaria, typhoid or meningitis even, searched his desk for some cash because the drugs would be expensive. But then he heard the doctor ask for boiling water and clean towels. His wife emerged from Leila's room and shut the door firmly, trying to slip past him. Mahmoud caught the pallor of panic in her face. He grabbed at her shoulder, roughly turning her towards him. She would not look him in the eye.

'What is it?' Mahmoud hissed at her. Something dreadful was congealing at the back of his mind. He studied his wife with loathing. She shrugged off his hands and moved towards the kitchen, saying, 'The doctor has told me to light the stove.'

Mahmoud sat on the black plastic ottoman, motionless, listening to the low voices that came from the bedroom. From time to time there was a girlish whimpering. Mahmoud's heart froze – and cracked.

When the doctor re-emerged from the bedroom, when he had done scribbling chits and prescriptions, he snapped his attaché case shut and looked at Mahmoud quizzically.

'I thought you had decided against all that?'

'All what?' asked Leila's father, his voice defiantly flat.

His wife came out, carrying away a pan of stained water. The doctor let his glance follow Mrs al-Haq a moment, then studied the father hunched on the ottoman. Mahmoud's face seemed to have lost all tone and all expression.

The doctor placed the prescriptions on the glass-topped table.

'Don't delay. It was total, Pharaonic, and badly done. There is a lot of infection. I'll be back tomorrow.'

Mrs al-Haq did wonder if her husband would kill her. But not only did he not raise a hand against her: he barely spoke at all. Leila kept her room for a week, and in the first four days Mahmoud did not talk with her, did not even go in. At last he sat on her bed and held her hand a minute, but looked out of the window.

His wife was not sure whether he was accepting defeat, or was brewing up to some cataclysmic rage in which she would be divorced. She was glad of the support of her friends who assured her that she had saved Leila from uncleanness and spinsterhood. In the meantime, if Mrs al-Haq were to need refuge . . .

At this, tears sprang into her eyes. How could she have landed the one husband in all Sudan who didn't care about his daughters' future? Who had no thought for the ignominy of the uncircumcised? For the misery of the unmarriageable? Didn't he love their girls?

The friends hushed and consoled her. Leila would soon be married, and if her father had a scrap of decency he would come to understand that Mrs al-Haq had acted properly.

But still Mahmoud said nothing. The mutilation could never be reversed. Protest and recrimination would merely dignify the atrocity, lifting it to a plane of rational debate where his wife could come out with travesties of justification. He did not want that, to listen to that, to hear *reasons* why his daughter should have her genitalia cut away. There was nothing left but sorrow. And, since his wife was out of sympathy, she would be excluded. This was his revenge.

So Leila came from her room, weakened, cured but not healed. Between her and her father, few words passed. But, a few days later, he took her to the airport. They went – just the two of them – to look at the jets. Boeings, Fokkers, Antonovs; two hundred, three hundred tonnes apiece. Father and daughter gazed at these astonishing vessels that rose from the squashy tarmac of Sudan and spread across the sky, across the modern world. Then they took a soft drink together and came home. As they re-entered the house, Leila saw her mother glare at her father and realized that the trip had been a sort of riposte, even a small victory.

Mahmoud still placed confidence in Khamisa, who grew into a young lady of quick intelligence and caustic wit. She won a place at the University Languages Faculty and suddenly there was ambitious talk in the house: of the senior Civil or Diplomatic Services, of posts abroad, a scholarship perhaps. Mrs al-Haq made little contribution to these discussions. Mahmoud did the speculating, Khamisa enjoyed the limelight and Leila watched, secretly perturbed by the sudden flux of her father's hopes.

When Khamisa became engaged to marry, announcing this within just two months of starting at the Languages Faculty, Mahmoud shrank from her in dread. A week later, Khamisa stopped attending the university. When her father asked why, she replied that it was her fiancé's wish. The young man was going to Saudi for a year; he preferred Khamisa to remain at home and she would certainly obey. Mahmoud stared as though mesmerized by a snake he thought he'd scotched. When he came to his senses, he began to protest – but Khamisa coldly reminded him of his own teachings: that their life's decisions were in their own hands, no one else's. Their mother gloried in every detail of the wedding plans from the day the engagement was announced, but Leila thought her father's spirit would never recover.

At sixteen, she was conscious that all those tremendous hopes now focused on her alone, and were a great burden.

Walking in the street with Mahmoud one day, a group of young men came towards them and Leila lowered her eyes. As soon as the men had passed, her father stopped, turned her by the shoulder and slapped her face.

As she gazed at him in mute astonishment, he snapped: 'You looked down! Why did you look down? Are they better than you? Are they worthier, are they some kings or presidents that my daughter must lower her eyes?'

She saw that he was trembling.

She became afraid; the more he believed that there

was nothing he could do of worth in this world, the more he placed that duty upon his Leila. If she had known some terms in which she could have remonstrated without wounding him still further, she'd have spoken. But her father was shrinking day by day. His health, his courage and his authority were failing, and it broke her heart to see. Three months after delivering that slap, he died suddenly.

Mrs al-Haq was principally distressed for her own financial position as a widow. But Leila's grief knew no end. And she kept Mahmoud's colour book of geography all her professional life.

YIN YANG

Bill Duncan

Grey sky glowers over tenements, like an underexposed photograph. The Nike bag crashes through the pub door: Malc. Just been for a haircut, his second in a fortnight. His hair was short before the first one, but he said it was better for the tae kwon do, the swimming, the mountain biking and the weight training. Also gave him the chance to tell me to 'Get rid o that pony-tail, ya poser,' again. Nobody believes Malc's got a forty-four inch chest and everybody knows he's under five feet seven, but nobody questions. When Malc sits down, he puffs himself out like one of these lizards that frightens off its enemies by looking twice as big as it really is. He takes up the space of three men, opening his legs to 135 degrees. Thank God Malc doesnae wear a skirt. Then there's the voice. No wonder they call Malc 'The One-Man-Crowd', but not to his face. Aye. The face. I'll leave that to one of the regulars: 'A bra' puss fur fleggin bairns.' He's been a wee bit touchy for the last quarter of a century. Dates back to the time he was asked to leave Uni. Malc buys one for himself, buys one for me, sits down.

'Cheers, Malc.'

'Awright, Cammy?'

'No bad, Malc. Yerself?'

Oh Christ. Here comes Midge, carrying an unidentified musical instrument case. Midge has an MA First Class Honours in Fine Art, a Ph.D in Early Renaissance Fresco and a B.Sc. in Molecular Biology. He plays saxophone, double bass, harpsichord, clarinet, French horn and the banjo. He has a forty-four inch chest and is six feet two. We call him 'The Three Degrees'. What bonds The One-Man-Crowd and The Three Degrees is a sado-masochistic relationship with Dundee United and a loathing of Jim McLean.

When Midge comes in Malc roars: 'Hey! Ya big useless bastard! You're late!'

'Fuck off.'

'Pint?'

'Fuck off.'

'What's the matter wi you, then?'

'—— —'

'Hey! What's the matter?'

'Wednesday.'

'Wednesday?'

'Yes. Wednesday.'

'You never turned up. I left training sharp. Got straight up here. Ask Frankie, Davie or Andy. Half six. Dead on. Gave you till six-forty. No sign. We had tae get tae East End Park, so . . .'

'I was here at half past six.'

'No.'

'*I was here at half past six.*'

'WERE YOU FUCK HERE AT HALF-SIX.'

Ally the barman pokes his head round the door. 'Midge, that's Caroline on the phone.'

'Right. Thanks Ally.'

Things often got like this with Malc and Midge. A

verbal sparring that came to be expected of them: part of their repertoire of male bonding rituals. We suspected some of the older guys came to the pub for these and other confrontations: the place was full of flytings where the two protagonists only ever came to verbal blows and which usually concluded with one of the combatants shouting 'Fuck off!' to the delight of the company, who understood the rules of engagement.

A couple of times recently, though, things had ended with the slamming of doors and pints left with only a couple of mouthfuls taken and folk staying away for a time. On one occasion, Malc stayed away for a week, Midge for a fortnight, prompting one of the regulars to say: 'No bein nosy, son but what aboot Malc an his big mate? Have they fawn oot?'

Malc was now a sprightly, sharp-looking forty-seven, with grey hair, but fit and in good condition, without enjoying particularly good health. Despite his training sessions and workouts, a cold could knock him out for a fortnight. But, being Malc, he was under pressure to maintain a reputation as an ex-hardman, an intellectual and an athlete.

Midge was forty-two; he and Caroline had just started a family with the twins and disposable income had fallen. This meant that Caroline got very pissed off when Midge still came home with obscure, expensive, specially ordered American Blues import CDs so he could learn the guitar solos which he played when he got home from the pub, waking up Caroline and the bairns.

Midge comes back from the phone, grateful that the pub is quiet, avoiding the grins and pitying headshakes that accompany the public humiliation of your wife phoning the pub. All he has to contend with is a knowing look from Malc, who senses it's better not to say anything too provocative.

'We've run out of disposable nappies. Remember the Garlic Nan with the takeaway. Be on time.'

Malc settles for, 'No easy bein the New Man, eh?'

Being 'that bit older' Malc felt none of the pressures on the rest of us to reflect recent styles in clothes and music. In fact, Malc liked to exaggerate the age difference, going for an 'elder statesman' role which involved wearing the occasional pair of desert boots, a cheesecloth shirt or, notably, a pair of light tan cowboy boots. When Malc wore these things they didn't display the subtly altered details which made them referential and self-conscious: the nineties looking back at the seventies. He simply wore out-of-date clothes quite happily. But nobody said anything. When Midge or any of the rest of us appeared in a linen jacket with a mandarin collar, talking about Portishead or The Stone Roses, Malc simply stated: 'Fuckin' forty-something stunted adolescent poofs.'

Things start to settle comfortably with Midge's return from the phone and the recent slump in United's form provides fairly safe ground. Malc pitches in with: 'The best thing McLean ever did was gettin rid of that big sand-dancin bastard. Four million for a Yahoo that goes on the pish eight nights a week an kicks the crutches away fae cripples in taxi queues.'

'Aye. But what about the four million? What have we got for strikers? One long-term injured an another long-term out of form. It's like the partially sighted leadin' the blind up front these days. An that prima donna in the mid-field. He's no interested. He's wantin away an it shows.'

'Naw.'

'No? What d'ye mean "no"?'

'Listen.' Malc lowers his voice, moves his eyes horizontally, scans the room, shifts his seat forward, so that we're instinctively drawn towards him. He continues: 'Frankie's brither's his next-door neighbour. He's no wantin away far United. Know the problem?'

'?'

'Waccy baccy. Drink. Snortin. Frankie says his brither says there's a court case next month. United want *him* away fae *them* . . .'

'Well no wonder the bugger's lost his form.'

'Aye. Quicker they get him doon tae England the better.'

'Aye. Take the money an run. An buy a decent striker with it.'

'Somethin else . . .'

'?'

'See that game he missed last week – *supposedly* through injury?'

'Yeah.'

'Injury my arse.'

'Eh?'

'Banjoed by a boy up in The Gun. Been carryin on wi a dame fae the multis. Her man comes home unannounced fae the rigs Friday night an caught yer man at it wi his wife. The brither-in-law bides next door tae the dame. Good-lookin bit stuff, tae.'

'Who? The brother-in-law?'

'Naw – the dame, ya smart bastard.'

'Right enough, I've thought he looked slower in the

tackle. Hardly surprisin if he's spendin the night before the game gettin his leg ower.'

'Aye. Well the sooner they get rid o the horny wee junky the better.'

Having managed to avoid anything too controversial the conversation fades and the potential silence is ruthlessly nailed by Midge, who moves his bottom jaw two inches to the left and states: 'See these two dames over there? They've spoke aboot *Brookside* and *Eastenders* for the past fifteen minutes. No real, eh? Fuckin soap opera. Fuckin women.'

All three of us turn to look at the women. Part of a foursome. The two women were still going hard at it about how Jimmy Corkhill was a nice fella really and what a shame it was for Arthur. Their men were engaged in a totally separate parallel discussion about how that Big Bastard wiz never fit tae lace Andy Gray's boots anyway.

'Fuckin women all right,' repeats Malc.

And at that precise instant two of them walk into the back-room. Young, student types, early twenties, though they couldn't look more different: the one who comes in first leaves the three of us sitting with our shoulders hunched and our jaws dropped. Black. Tall. Long shiny hair, purple lipstick, high cheekbones and tight black stuff. Jesus. Her pal shorter, spiky fair hair, long denim dress and sandshoes. The tall one stands at the bar ordering her drinks as we silently try not to stare. She senses our unease and does what comes naturally. She smiles. A great big facesplitter, her cheekbones riding so high they close her eyes for a second.

'Hello.'

Time hangs for an instant as she stands smiling,

framed by the winter sunset glowing through the frosted-glass window. Her wee spiky pal comes back from the Ladies, joins her at the bar and helps her to carry their drinks. They sit down two tables away and start talking.

Malc recovers. 'Who the fuck does the big glamorous one think she is tae come in here and look at us like that, eh?'

'Some lookin woman, though, eh, Malc?' Midge offers.

I settle for, 'Ach, women are different these days, especially the young student types. Anyway, good to see some new faces in the pub, eh?'

Midge is clearly unconvinced. Time to change the subject.

'How's the Housing Office, Malc?'

'Aw, Jesus, man. Crazy. This town's gettin worse. Ye heard about the horse?'

'The horse?'

'Aye.'

'No a horse.'

'I'm tellin ye – a horse. We were lookin fur a horse. We're still lookin fur it.'

'But . . . a horse?'

'Aye. Every time the bastard moonlighted, he took the horse wi him. Oh aye, we had heard o it all right. But I didnae believe it. No until I saw it wi my ain eyes – canterin along the landin, bold as fuck, wi yer man joggin alongside. The Horseman o Happyhillock.'

'Jesus.'

'Aye. An that's no all. Oh no. Other bastard had a livin room full of tatties.'

'Naw.'

'Aye. The man wiz movin hoose. Our man wiz checkin the place oot. Jist seein all the doors an that were still there, right?'

'Aye.'

'Well, yer man's fine – nice as ninepence. A braw wee fella – polite an co-operative an that. Until our man asks yer man if it's OK tae check out the livin room. Then yer man gets a bit, shifty, sayin, "Naw, it's awright, like, there's nae need." So our man gets kinda suspicious. Know whut Ah mean?'

'Aye.'

'So, our man says tae yer man, "Look, sir, it's oor right tae see intae a yer rooms. We'll huv tae insist on this. It's in the regulations." Well, yer man's lookin kind o sheepish like, an when they go intae the livin room know whut they see?'

'Tatties?'

'Aye. The hail fuckin flair, wall tae wall, covered in black polythene wi big fuckin tattie sha's stickin oota the holes. Ceilin covered in big fluorescent strips. A field o'tatties. In a hoose.'

'Jesus.'

'Aye. An see yesterday – out in Mid-Kirkfield. Ye'll no believe this. Checkin this boy's house. The livin room. Forty chairs, set out in rows, facin a wee stage aw din up in pink velvet. Now what dae you think went oan on that stage?'

'Jesus. That just aboot beats the lot, Malc.'

'Right enough. But our line o work ye see folk at their weirdest. Some mad things goin on out in the schemes. Did ye read aboot the Hen Killings?'

'Eh?'

'The Hen Killings. Up in Blackfield.'

'No.'

Malc picks up the evening paper, opens it and reads aloud the following item:

'DEAD HENS MYSTERY

Mystery surrounds the gruesome discovery of the partially burned bodies of six hens on a disused road bordering Dundee's Blackfield estate.

The bodies of the six birds were found by Blackfield Avenue resident Thomas Douglas as he walked his dog in Pitkerr Road.

Three black hens had been left at the side of the road – two had their legs chopped off. The charred remains of the three beheaded white hens were lying in the ashes of a bonfire.

"I think the fire was lit on Tuesday night," said Mr Douglas. "My wife noticed a smell of burning and heard laughter and squawking. I went to investigate but I couldn't see anyone."

Dundee District Council Environmental Health Department has been alerted. A spokesman from Tayside Police advised householders in the area to exercise especial vigilance over their hens: "Whoever did this could strike again."'

Malc finishes his story as Midge reflects: 'Aye, the place is goin daft right enough. The sister lives up the North End an hasnae been sleepin that well lately. Been wakened up by gunfire most weekends. Never makes the papers, like, but there's folk drunk, stoned an runnin aboot wi guns up there.'

'Aye. Fun an games all right,' observes Malc.

Just at that moment the beautiful one, who has been

paying a lot of attention to the stories, strides across to the bar. Her face lights up as she says to Ally: 'Excuse me, could you change this fiver for pound coins?'

The Jamaican accent turns a few more heads. Now there's only two things that take pound coins in this place. One of them is the condom machine in the men's toilet. The other is the condom machine in the women's toilet. We couldnae believe it when Ally got it put in. Caroline was in one night and when she came back from the Ladies she was impressed. Said it showed that at last the place was movin' into the 1970s. I agreed with her and thought it sounded sensible enough, what with the HIV problem and that.

Midge shrugged and said he had lost the place with modern relationships and couldnae work out who the hell was supposed to be makin the running and was glad to be settled down because it was all too fucking complicated anyway. Then he shrugged and took a huge draw on his pint.

Malc was horrified. But he was being horrified more and more often these days. The last time was the previous Friday when some students came in on their way to a party – happy and dressed to break yer heart. Exuberant, young, out for a good time and letting the world know. Some of the women were beautiful, knew it and weren't hiding it. Amongst the predominating denim, harlequin Pringle V-necks, polyester anoraks and greying, thinning hair, the perfume, black lycra, swirling dreadlocks and bare skin made an impression. Malc had a hard job coping and muttered darkly about wishing the pub had stayed the same. Now he's lost for words again as the beautiful one says brightly: 'Thank you – just for the machine!'

'What d'ye think o that? Fur Chrissake! Buyin con-
doms in the pub! Bold as brass and claes like that! Askin
fur it! *Askin fur it!*'

I stare down at my black suede Doc Martens. Midge
shuffles nervously and the spiky one shoots Malc a
glance that lowers his voice. Midge swiftly drains his
pint, asking: 'Same again, then?' as I make my way to
the men's toilet.

My path back is blocked when I stumble into the
beautiful one coming out of the Ladies with a couple
of exotic-looking shiny packets between her thumb and
forefinger. I apologize awkwardly and she smiles
broadly. I find it hard not to stare as she hands the
packets to her pal saying: 'Here, Jenny, have a good
time tonight, though I can't work out what you see in
these damned males!'

'Ach, you an your sisters, Marilyn. It's no my scene
any more.'

Both of them laugh into their drinks as the wee one
casts an ironic glance in the direction of us: 'Some are
better than others, right enough!'

Luckily Malc and Midge miss this passage of play as
Midge returns to the table with three pints and Malc is
starting another story. 'Two weeks ago. Up in Baltic
Foods. Boy next tae me in the Housin Office knows the
lad that found him. Poor bastard wiz blue an stiff by
then. That wiz on the Monday. Him an a bunch o his
pals had gone up tae The Gun fur a bevvy Friday dinner
time. They'd been on time an a half for two nights on
the cabbages. Seems the boy wiz right on form, up on
the Karaoke, givin *Please Release Me* laldy. The lot
of them were half pissed by the time they got back an
they were a fuckin aboot among the vegetables. Well

yer man wiz actin the goat in the Cold Store an that's where it went wrang. Seems like he thought it wid be a clever idea tae go hidin fae the others in the upright freezer. Couldnae get oot. Poor bugger starts bangin an roarin, but you know whut it's like inside one o these things – great big bastard o a vacuum seal, nae chance o screams gettin oot. By this time yer man's goin aff the heid, but a his mates are gettin seek o the nonsense an clearin up tae go back tae The Gun. What happens is yer man's panickin that much that he cowps the freezer ower on its back. Juist like a great big white freezin coffin. Now yer man lived on his own an often went away fur the weekend, so naebody thought ony mair o it. Monday. That wiz when the first shift came in an they knew something wiz wrang. Fur a start, he wiz usually first man in. When they went intae the Cold Store an saw the freezer lyin on its back, well . . . the boy opens the freezer door and there's yer man starin up wi a face on him like somethin oot a fuckin horror film. The poor bastard who found him near ended up in Intensive Care, wi his jabberin an shakin an a thing. Funeral's next Tuesday up at the Crem.'

'That'll thaw the puir bugger oot,' says Midge.

'Nae mair nonsense in the Cold Store,' concludes Malc.

As Malc finishes his story, the young women finish their drinks, rise and call over to us: 'Bye, lads, and thanks for the entertainment.'

'Yeah! Thanks! That was great. Maybe see you again, boys!'

Midge hesitates, lost for words. Malc reaches for a parting shot, but can find only: 'Aye . . . well. Cheerio then . . .'

And they're gone.

Minutes later Malc is still shaking his head as I sit down beside him with three pints. 'Good fuckin riddance tae the pair of them – one a lesbian an the ither a flamin maneater!'

'Aye, but, Midge, but could you guess which one was which?'

Taking a long draw on his pint, Malc's eyes widen over the top of his glass. 'Eh?'

He stares in deepening horror at the side of my face which has been turned away from him until now, his face twisted in disbelief. 'Jesus . . ' he gasps, almost choking on the beer he has barely swallowed, spraying flecks of foam across the table. 'No! No an ear-ring. Naw! No pierced ears. Aw, Cammy!' Malc splutters, focusing on my left ear and the small yin-yang symbol I've been wearing for the last few days.

THE CLIENT

John Cunningham

Tall moustached Gillespie with veiled brown eyes managed, and still manages, the chemical company for which Tony hauled. George Gillespie was, and is, his biggest client.

Tony ate dinner left by his wife in the kitchen and lit a cheroot and walked across a concreted yard from the house to the office occupying the front of the oldest garage.

'Where's Cyril?'

Martha plucked a sheet from her machine and frowned at it before answering: 'Away in the van to Ayr for something.'

He stroked a sore that had recently appeared at the side of his mouth and gazed at the blackboard on the wall showing the work of his lorries that day, without seeing it, and ignoring the papers she'd put on his desk.

'When'll he be back?'

'Didn't say.'

He sat ten minutes, and tapped a phone number: 'George?'

'Tony! What can I do for you?'

The voice, replayed in his head, sounded normal.

'Eighteen-tonner tomorrow morning, that okay is it?'

'Have we a problem?' Gillespie queried.

'No, fine . . . checking up. And, eh . . .' he detailed
another five lorries due to pick up at the Chemical
company next day and replaced the phone. Martha sat
a little stiffly and raised her crafty face from the
machine to glance innocently at him. She knew and
the boys in the workshop and drivers knew, sleekit and
respectful of his unseen disease; they all knew.

'He say when he'd be back?'

She looked exasperated and shook her head.

He walked into the yard with clenched fists and splat-
tered Gillespie's head against the wall, punched till the
mouth was red pulp, teeth mixed with moustache, his
knuckles bruised and cut. He prowled at the side of
the office hoping Cyril would not be long. He couldn't
go in with Martha and he drifted to the garage adopting
a stern look as he entered its high tin doors. A vehicle
stood on the oil-stained floor for servicing before it
went to be plated yet no-one was about, where the hell
– but instead of striding to the workshop he stopped
behind the garage door.

He wanted to see the kids when they came home
from school. What could he do in the house that would
seem normal? They were used to him being at the garage all day and only regularly in the house at meal
times. What could he be doing? The stamps, that was
it!

He crossed the yard looking straight ahead, wiped
his shoes and hung up his jacket, took the Stanley Gib-
bons from behind the glass ornaments and laid it in
front of him on the coffee table in the living room,
having left the door open. He'd treasured this album
when he was young. But he'd forgotten it, till Ann sug-
gested David might be interested and, several winters

ago, they'd bought packets of new stamps, replaced dried-out hinges and even renamed pages, so many countries' names had changed. Without ever being sure how interested David was, he'd enjoyed it and now though it was a ploy he was engrossed by the triangular Mozambique ones, forgetting what he was doing and who he was.

It had started with an old Commer, kept in the road. His father shod horses like his father before him but Tony saw where the future lay. He worked hard and put a new vehicle on the road running to England while the Commer worked Ayr and Kilmarnock. Then he'd levelled the ground behind the smithy with ballast from the railway that Dr Beeching had closed and took a loan to build a garage. He and Cyril would sit up there on fine mornings with a pocketful of nuts and bolts, legs dangling, cladding the roof-frame and seeing ships out by Arran. The smithy was now stacked with steel, its old wooden door rotted in the nettles. His father'd come out with a hot shoe in pincers since the horses – now riding ponies – who'd used to stand in the forge while stars from the anvil died on the earth floor around their feet, were tethered outside, away from welding torches.

He had met Ann in a bar in Torremolinos when he was thirty-two years old. For a hectic period thereafter weekends were spent in Norfolk; down there he met her folks and her friends, different people. The dad was an easy-going chap in a family firm, they'd come down from Ayrshire in the twenties. He simply wondered at its easiness in the sunny dark-beamed house smelling of high-quality furniture polish.

Back home Father died and Ina who'd kept house

for them wanted away. Even before the wedding he had begun adding to the house where he'd been born, a porch, a double-glazed picture window and a garage. When Ann came she did it over, new kitchen, new curtains, new wallpaper and paint, and he was proud, in the front room with a beer, while she cooked a simple meal. They went out and had friends in. Had a memorable house-warming. Out the window was the enormous view. And he saw, squarely, that he'd be one of the biggest if not the biggest haulier in Ayrshire. He'd always tended to forget her part in it. She'd taken over book-keeping when Martha said she didn't mind a wee rest, and reorganized the office and become a partner – part of himself, he saw it, blind to it being the part that came up with good ideas, including the chemical company, Gillespie.

They would start early. Sometimes he'd leave her and work in the garage. And when she looked at him a certain way they'd call Cyril to watch the phone and nip back to the house.

After David was born she was in the office less, and after Ruth she stopped altogether; and he'd coaxed Martha back.

Business chugged along, he knew how a day would go. After a number of years he had twenty on the road and was looking for more yet. It was hard to see what it had been like not long ago. An aluminium-clad workshop dwarfed the smithy; David was into second year at High School and Ruth had started there – that was when he discovered Ann was two-timing him. There wasn't a particular moment; the tide had seeped round him and he was up to his neck. He could see nothing else. An oddness in people's manner – pause, extra look. Couldn't speak to anyone without seeing it.

He had forced himself to ask her one evening, damned awkwardly as he remembered, about this fellow, this older man who moved in a different circle, Gillespie. Oh, she met him lots of places, tennis, whist drives; she admitted she liked George and told him it was his own fault she'd found someone she 'liked to talk to', who was amusing, since he himself wouldn't take her out. She'd carried it off, hell mend her, and he hadn't pressed.

Ruth came off the bus, waved to her friends and he heard her in the door by the time David swooped through the gate on his twelve-gear racer, sweating, big tongues of his trainers sticking up; came head-down over the yard and checked his watch at the door. From the unusual viewpoint of the house Tony for no reason felt sorry for him; there was no reason, he was doing fine at school, but Tony felt desperately sorry for him.

'Hi, Dad.' She didn't let on she thought it strange him being in the house, and looked at him with twelve-year-old wisdom. Too late, too late. He'd missed stages of her that wouldn't come again because he'd been so damn busy; and was grateful she stood beside him in white shirt, loosened lopsided tie and school skirt and watched the pages as he turned them, with him, not saying anything. Then she took a glass of juice and her homework upstairs and he heard her music.

David peeked round the door, red-faced, and came over with a soft grin. 'Hullo there. That's great.'

'What, the stamps?'

'Yeah.'

He caught his son's eye. It was not blank but full of

confusion and understanding. He looked away quickly. When he peeked up David had gone; his shoes had squeaked on the lino in the passage and he was calling from the kitchen, 'Tea, Dad?'

He shouted back yes.

'Where's Mum?'

'Don't know.'

David brought him a mug and went to the TV in the kitchen. He had not expected David to have stayed and talked. He wouldn't have known what to say. They'd never talked except when he'd instructed the boy about something. He turned pages, but it had died in his hands and might as well go to the jumble. He heard Cyril's van and hurried out, in case he should meet her too returning.

They unloaded boxes of filters. They rolled a forty gallon drum of oil from the back of the van on to a tyre, with a squelch and a thump when the rim none the less hit concrete, trundled it to a corner and set it up.

He wiped his hands and said gruffly, 'Have a word before you go home.' Cyril nodded and went into the store to do paperwork while Tony smoked and watched a driver clean his rig. He knew it got on their tits, his recent habit of watching, but couldn't help it. The pressurized jet hissed and drummed on the windscreen, sluiced the green cab and rippled. 'A. GRAY' in the circle of address and phone number, and the water ran down oily concrete to the drain. Past the cab, half a mile away, crows circled yellowing trees and the spire poking up among them. Ann took the Brownies in the church hall there. And over the town because it was a clear day he saw a cloud merged with sea hiding the

lower half of Arran and trailing away in a long scarf to
the south. Goat Fell and the Castles rose above it, the
Sannox Burn a dull streak like old snow. He drew breath
and gulped the smell of his cheroot in the cool air.
Nights would be drawing in, clocks changing, stags roaring, lights twinkling across the water by four o'clock.
He took a turn through the workshop while hoses were
coiled and doors locked.

Martha, shrugging her coat comfortably over broad
shoulders: 'Here's letters for signing. Thought you'd
have been in and done them sooner and I could have
put them in the post on my road home.'

'I'll see to them, Martha.'

'That's me away.' She looked at them. They'd all
been at school together.

'Right, Martha.'

They heard her footsteps in the yard. Cyril was doing
the last thing before going home, chalking up the blackboard for the next day.

Tony noted the falling dusk. At about this time
people who'd spent the afternoon together would come
out from some place or other up or down the coast, a
flat, a cottage, a hotel, and start back to their homes,
and in a short while would have reached them, as if
nothing whatever had happened. He saw her in the
kitchen as she would be when he went in, cooking.
Cooking, in her mind, for him! Gillespie could have
left his office immediately after that phone call, perhaps
a little anxious and wondering why he'd called, but . . .
it was foul. He imagined her slowly taking off her dress
in the afternoon. The chalking of the board continued
in a different time zone. Nearly all the work was for the
chemical company. He saw her pulling on tights, easing

her feet into shoes, in a way he knew, in a room he'd
never seen. He could take no more of it.

'Aaaahh! HAD ENOUGH!' And he'd flung the ash-
tray, glass splinters over the floor, his face stuck in
Cyril's.

Cyril pushed him off. 'Okay, okay, man, you scared
shit out of me! What the hell . . . Sit down, eh?' And
he'd pushed him into his chair and taken Martha's,
swivelling it round.

Tony, mouth agape, jaw thrust out: 'All I can take!
Ann and that bugger! Had all I can bloody take and I
tell you – I don't want to know more about it!' He
lunged at the board, wiped it clean. 'Fuck 'em!'

'You can't do that, Tony!'

'How can't I?!'

'Ach, well . . .'

'Gillespie can look elsewhere for his transport! I'll
do what I like, it's my business.' He pointed at Cyril. 'I
can put the lorries down the road tomorrow! Wash my
hands of it. Phone call's all it needs!'

'Eh?' There was silence, Cyril's eyes widened. 'You're
off your head! Ah well, if that's the way of it . . .'

Tony insisted, 'I tell you: fellow's been at me a
while.'

Cyril was frightened at his friend's blank face. He
looked at the floor, elbows on knees, looked at the floor
and rubbed the knuckles dangling between the knees
and muttered, 'That's all right then.'

Tony sprang from the chair. 'What d'you mean all
right? Hell m'n, I know you're thinking of your job! I
said down the road but he'll take it as a going concern,
no jobs'll be lost. I want no more of it.'

'And what'll folk think of you?'

Tony hmpphed. He sat down: 'You seen 'em? Know where they go?'

'Ah, look, Tony –'

'I said have you seen 'em!!'

Cyril said vaguely enough for it to sound like specu-lation, scratching his head, 'Ach, they passed me this afternoon on the Ayr road . . . but . . . I don't –'

'She needn't think she's coming back. She's made me a laughing stock and I'm chucking her out – I'll kill him!' He stuck out his chin.

Cyril almost sniggered and pretended not to have. He muttered 'Aye, aye,' and looked at the floor, seeing that if Ann went, and took Gillespie, they'd all be down the drain, and after a while he asked bluntly, 'Where'd she go, d'you think?'

Tony heard the tick of the clock, rescued from the school when the alterations were done. The big hand had used to take forever getting through forty minutes and the wonky thing still seemed only just to manage the up-side. His glance met Cyril's. 'What'll I do?'

'Have you talked to her?'

'Not really. Won't do any good.'

'Eh – give me one of those, eh.'

Tony offered the packet, flicked the lighter, watched Cyril expel smoke and wrinkle his nose.

'See,' Cyril said, 'you know Gillespie, he's a jack-rabbit, think back, eh, you don't know how many he's been through – only thing'd stop him's castration. So it's odds on – I know what you're feeling – not that he's been at my missus far as I know – an insult when you think of it – the bugger, eh – but he's not – I mean he's never long satisfied and he'll be looking round and twitching his nose for a new one soon, you'll see.

But he's a dangerous sod. If you bawled him out he could . . .'

'So what'm I do to, nothing?!'

'Ach, I know what you're going through.'

'You've no idea!'

'Hell, I'm doing my best.'

'What do I do then?'

'In your shoes I'd hang on.' Cyril studied the end of the black cheroot and laid it on the desk. 'Gillespie'll blow by. And you don't want him getting the better of you. Do you? Now, if he was one of the wee guys we do an odd job for you could tell him to get lost – but he's not, eh? You've got to admit, he could put us in a right pickle. You've to think of that. It's not just myself, it's all of us and you too – hell's sake, if you fly up and tell him to find another haulier, he will! You could maybe, to ease your mind, let Ann know you know what's going on – but you'll not need to lose the rag.'

Tony turned the problem all ways, bothering the side of his mouth with the tip of his finger. Courses of action resolved to one; Cyril was right. He clasped his hands behind his head and articulated a small nod.

Cyril had swiftly popped the dead cheroot in his pocket. 'I'll sort that in the morning,' he said of the blackboard and broken glass. He zipped his jacket and felt for the piece bag at his feet. 'Mind now,' he said, leaving, watching closely, 'don't do anything I wouldn't.'

He stared at nothing. He heard the car and peered out and saw it draw up at the house. He saw Ann get out and go in the back door. Her affair with Gillespie was as real as the house, the car.

He would shortly go in for his tea, into the kitchen

when they were at table and they would know that something had changed. Next time he spoke with Gillespie
on the phone he would know too. They might accident-
ally meet somewhere. George, he might say . . .

She would be checking what she'd left in the low
oven and putting things on the table with the quick
skill of years. He harked back to the early days when it
was her business too. Oh, now a sad business! Lying at
the edge of the bed not speaking because her being
Gillespie's lover couldn't be allowed over the door of
the house let alone the sill of the bedroom . . . once
he'd talked to her perhaps it would change? It wasn't
too different to being about to go into hospital for
major surgery – by the morning it would be done. He
didn't know how he'd feel but the business would be
intact and everyone's job. For the business, he told
himself.

Outside the window a cloud of gnats rose and fell in
the light and he wished he knew their method of living
and surviving frosts. He left the blackboard for Cyril.
He gripped the letters and envelopes ready for the post
in one hand and with the other doused the light and
locked the door. Noticing his hands at these jobs without his consciousness and seeing on them familiar scars,
he felt ready as he could be. He crossed the yard, in
through the back, dumped the letters. With his hand
on the door knob he imagined David and Ruth at table;
Ann turning from the stove, her eyes shining yet.

TO KILL A FISH

Anthony Lambert

His knife for the big hen lobster might have been a just exchange, though probably not in McAfferty's eyes. As it was, he ended up with neither. He was having a bad day.

It had started indirectly in the pub the previous evening. The boys had been roasting him over his obtuse pride in the possession, next to the alarm clock at his bedside, of an old MW-LW wireless. It had been his grandfather's and he liked it for its mock walnut case and thick fat knobs and the warm dusty smell from it as the valve glowed and came alive, but it was beyond him to explain it and so he'd simply endured the crack. 'Did you never hear of such a thing as a radio alarm, man? Give you Malin and Hebrides without even opening your eyes, and by the time he gets to Fair Isle and Faroes, if there's no weather for it, you can be sinking right back into the old Irish Sea.' The not quite meaningless jest had angered McAfferty and he'd been still angry enough, when he went to bed, to overwind the clock, wringing its guts tight as those of a drawn cockerel. His own inner alarm had let him down by a few critical moments and by the time he'd tuned the old wireless it was nine nine four and falling at Butt of Lewis. McAfferty had missed the shipping forecast.

That left him with the less precise prognosis from the previous night's TV picture. Developing low, freshening southwesterlies later. Leaving his anchorage in the late October dawn, the sea in his wake a rippling patchwork quilt of turquoise, jet and tangerine, McAfferty had harkened to the very first stirrings of the breeze; rounding the dark lump of the Toe he'd found the sea bumping him already, not rudely but nevertheless with a message in it, and the underside of the thickening cloudbase had taken on a dull cigar-brown hue, as if the sky already grudged its brilliant earlier show.

McAfferty hadn't liked it. Though he sensed no real malevolence in the signs, the six a.m. forecast was part of his routine, summer and winter, and its absence from the beginning of the day had unsettled him. The feeling hadn't eased. As he'd shifted his first fleet away from Rubha Dubh, a guano-covered rockface that McAfferty knew by a coarser name, the chop from a tidal cross-current had caused the top tier of his stack of creels to topple into the well of the boat. Restacking them McAfferty had, unusually for him, lost the sequence and subsequently shot the creels out of order, taking the leader rope into a tangle and jamming a loop of it around the rope guide, a steel pin bolted upright through the gunwale.

This had unsettled him the more. McAfferty knew every inch of his boat: the sealed knots in the planking that were now weathering a little, the crack in the second stern board, the carefully filled indentation three-quarters forward, just below the hauler, where he'd dug out a spot of rot; he knew the other weak points, too: the place in the gunwale where water had seeped in alongside an old fixture bolt hidden under a timber fillet and caused a second small area of decay; the nails that were drawing a little at the transom; the trio of worn ribs where oak had yielded slightly to prolonged contact with the steel bars of the creels. In his mind the worn ribs, the gunwale hole and the transom fixings formed a kind of triangle of potential weakness centred on the rope guide. He'd had a dream in which he'd been shooting gear at full speed to escape a storm and a jam on the rope guide had strained his boat so hard that the weight of the creels on the bottom had pulled the nails and snapped the weak timbers, taking out half the gunwale and all the planking on that quarter, clean down to the waterline. It was not a nice dream.

But this was a day not of disaster but of simple vexation, of mishaps and tangles. For the rope leader had only been the precursor; after that it was his fishing line, obstinately curling up on itself again and again as McAfferty, short of bait, fished with scant success for saithe and mackerel in the feeding grounds at the point. He'd pricked his fingers and lost a full trace and both his spare sinkers to the snatch of kelp as his boat drifted over it in the fierce tidal race, and then he'd imprudently weighted his line with the three-quarter-inch spanner he used for bleeding the injectors on the old Lister and lost that, too. Finally, with only a couple of saithe and a dozen or so mackerel left in his bait box and his ear more keenly tuned than usual to the regular thump of the idling engine, McAfferty had lost his bait knife as well.

It was the big hen. Cutting bait as he waited for the next creel of the fleet he was working, McAfferty had allowed his gaze to wander, following the leader, waiting for the first glimpse of the catch, for a consoling hint of the deep indigo blue that marked a carapace or upper tail, or the pale coral pink of a claw-underside. But this hen, when he saw her, was perched right in the open eye, arrested on her way in, or out, by the unaccustomed motion. McAfferty grabbed; too late, he remembered the knife in his hand, saw it shimmy down, handle first, and disappear into the kelp. The sight of it checked him an instant and the hen gave a convulsive flick of her berried tail and was gone from right under his hand, down, down, where he could never follow.

He swore then. Judging by the size of her the lobster would just about have paid for a new knife, at current prices. But he'd lost both. He seized the empty creel from the hauler sheaves and threw it, unbaited, at the others. At once the untidy lie of it became a reproach to him, to all that his livelihood depended upon. He straightened it then reached under the tiny open cuddy forward that saved him the worst of the drenchings that his boat took in a head wind. From the locker there he retrieved the knapsack in which he kept his flask and pieces.

'Take it easy, boy,' he said to himself, aloud. 'Time to take it easy, now.'

He checked that the gear remaining on the bottom gave him sufficient anchorage weight then sat down on the engine box, drinking coffee and smoking. Everything was wrong. It wasn't only his failure to catch the forecast. Normally his freezer was well stocked with fish or else his salting barrel was full, and he'd have enough frozen or salt bait stowed away in a polystyrene box in the locker to counter any disappearance of live fish from the point. Normally he wouldn't have dreamed of risking any of his engine tools at the end of a thin nylon trace. Normally his knife stayed strictly below gunwale height. These were the sensible, self-imposed rules of his occupation, learned the hard way. It seemed he was growing careless; a symptom, he guessed, of a wider and gathering disaffection.

He spat a tobacco shred into the sea. Here, in a shallow bay sheltered by a reef under the lighthouse that marked the point, the water was unruffled; not flat calm but glassy for all that, with a slow periodic back-surge that lifted the boat in a not unpleasant manner. He watched as the shred drifted by alongside, next to a little blob of jelly banded internally with reds and greens. The sun came out for a moment, and McAfferty saw the coloured bands of the tiny jellyfish take on an iridescent glow in the greeny depthless-looking columns of water. He scowled at it. It was too late in the year for a fancy show.

He saw a kink in the coiled leader rope and straightened it automatically. Tangles were the worst. He had an abhorrence of them. In his mind they were somehow connected with the tangle of his own genealogy. His maternal grandfather had been a tacksman, an incomer whose leases had blown right away in the reforms to leave him with only one small vacant croft gifted him by the laird. His grandmother, a servant in the big house, had also come from without. Her voice, always in demand for the ceilidh, had been the stuff of legend, but scandalmongers had whispered that her voice wasn't the only thing with which she was free and that the croft wasn't the only thing to be gifted his grandfather. McAfferty's mother, who sang only in church, had seldom spoken of her. His mother had two younger brothers: one had died in the war, the other had emigrated, but McAfferty had seen their photographs and there was something ill-boding about the lack of family resemblances.

His paternal side was no less of a mystery. His father, a ship's engineer, had come up with a coal puffer from somewhere mysteriously south of the Clyde, met and married his mother and gotten work locally on the ferries. McAfferty's first ever memory of the tug of a fishing line and the sweet vibration of a fish running with the darrow had his father firmly in the foreground. But only in the earliest years had it been good and it became a standing joke in the community that every time his father went to sea he came back with more of a roll to him. Nevertheless, McAfferty might have asked him face to face about his background, but one dark night when he was thirteen years old his father's first love had called and his seaman's roll had taken him out of the bar of the Norseman over to where the coal puffer happened to be lying again at berth, and one stumble too many found him floating later in the gap between her steel plates and the dock piling.

For her own reasons his mother, craving only the acceptance and support of her community and isolated from her own relatives, had thereafter refused all contact with his father's. McAfferty understood that his surname was a mis-spelling of something more common but in school a handful of spiteful peers had said it was an Irish name, instigating the taunts echoed the previous night in the pub. He had nothing against the Irish, who were a fine-voiced people like his mother's strain; still the jibes stung more than ever now, underlining as they did his peculiar lack of personal history. His own brother and sister, content to let him be the one to stay, were busy elsewhere putting years of poverty behind them in the pursuit of middle-class lifestyles and did not want to know. If there was a tangle he was in it, alone and for ever.

McAfferty threw away the butt end of his roll-up and considered the position. He hated the thought of going home with nearly half his gear unlifted, but he couldn't fish many more creels without bait. He glanced down at the recently segmented mackerel which would be the last ever to feel the cutting edge of his lost knife. The front part of it was still quivering as if it was trying to swim, as if it remained half in the world. It wouldn't quiver for long. It didn't take much, he thought, to kill a fish.

He felt no pity for it. A few aspects of a fisherman's life he did find disconcerting, like when he gaff-hooked a saithe and the delicate skin of its flank tore, the shimmering golds and silvers and khaki-greens peeling back to reveal little freshets of blood starting on the pink twill of the exposed muscle fibres. But mostly fishing was simply his job of work, and he just got on with it.

And today he'd made a proper cock-up of it. McAfferty knew, or rather felt, that there was a deeper root nurturing his disaffection. Though it preoccupied him increasingly it was hardly something that could be talked about openly. He wanted to be married. Since his mother's death, more than a year before, the house had been empty. For a long while it had been filled by the tyranny of possessive widowhood, then it had been filled by the more impersonal tyranny of illness; now it was just a shell. Where was a corner of it that was not empty? On Mondays McAfferty talked with the shellfish buyer and went to the shops, Tuesdays he nodded to a neighbour as he wheeled the garbage bin down, and midweek, Wednesdays or Thursdays, and again on Saturdays, he went to the pub for a few drams, though only a few, for some obstinate sense of his own worth prevented him from going the way of so many younger sons. But otherwise, when he wasn't fishing, McAfferty sat alone at home, a TV dinner on his knees. The only living things his hands touched were destined shortly to die. Fishing solo was one thing, bearable, perhaps even desirable. But living alone was quite another.

He turned, glancing over his shoulder as a movement caught his eye. McAfferty was habituated to watching the shipping in the Minch. It was as if he was half expecting something; a glimpse of the *Catriona B* perhaps, steaming out from the scrapyard, looking out of the dreich days to make manifest his dismay. But it was only the outward-bound Western Isles ferry plying her criss-cross route, stitching up the open channel like a resutured wound.

It ought to rain, he thought. The wind still had too much of the summer in it. As if to underline his thoughts he noticed a stray bee on his pieces' wrapper alongside, feasting on a stray blob of Co-op jam. McAfferty raised his hand reflexively, then let it fall. If the bee were to correct its error it would need all the energy-giving sweetness it could suck. Even if it made it back to shore the winter gales would hammer it soon enough. The seasons would break it in the way everything, in its time, was broken by them.

He tried to shrug off his melancholia. Still only in his mid-forties, McAfferty knew himself to be not that much past his prime and if a certain diffidence kept him from rejoinders and real repartee in the pub, he nevertheless had his relationships. Sometimes he talked aloud to the expected guests of his creels, the lobsters he wooed with such ardour, the ponderous brown crabs, the fierce little velvet crabs. 'Here's a change of menu, boys,' he might say with a sudden gruff unsentimental cheeriness as he baited-up with a small flat-fish that had strayed into his gear. 'Here's a wee bit plaice now, for your tea.' He cursed the bait-thieving gulls for vermin but sometimes, when he tossed them scraps of fish liver, they were 'lads'. The long-necked cormorants fanning themselves on the guano-splashed cliffs, the darting little terns, the puffins, the flashy gannets, though all more remote and uninterested in his daily passage and not much remarked upon by him, were all nevertheless part of it too, his society.

Away from the sea the spaces were filled mostly in a two-dimensional way by the newsreaders, the soap-opera and sitcom characters, or the weather forecasters. McAfferty especially liked it when it was Suzanne Charlton in front of the charts, he liked to watch the way the freshly shampooed bob of her hair swung behind her whenever she turned, like the glossy neatly coiffed tail of a shire mare at an agricultural show. But as soon as he thumbed the switch the corner of the room that housed the TV became the emptiest of all.

The problem was, of course, that there were few eligible women in his community now who might be willing to look at him. The visiting nurse who'd tended his ailing mother was single and there'd been a kind of awkwardness on the several occasions when he'd sat her down afterwards to take a cup with him, an awkwardness in being alone together that was no altogether unpleasant in the silent messages it conveyed. But in the end he'd let it slip, for as well as being kind and pleasant and trim with it, if no longer in her newest paint, she was teetotal and religious and McAfferty, who hadn't been in church since the funeral, was unsure that he could adapt his ways to the demands which her pious words of encouragement already had hinted at. Besides with her there might be heightened difficulties, he'd felt, with the protocols. Sighing, he replaced his flask and opened the control valve on the hauler.

He watched as creel after creel came up with little to show, and thought dourly that it might not make a lot of difference to leave the day half finished. The fishing was marginal now, the grounds knackered by chancers and incomers, Sassenachs with fat redundancy cheques and fancy boats and unlifted gear clogging the better marks. Out of the corner of his eye he glimpsed a basking shark swim slowly up to circle him curiously in the shallow margins of the bay. It was late in the year for a basker and the sight of the big plankton-eater brought a strange confusion to him. It had such a calm assurance about its place in the scheme of things, like the crews of the boats that sometimes crossed the Minch seeking an improved shellfish market, soft-spoken Hearachs of impeccable pedigree in whose company he felt sometimes exalted, sometimes more than ever deprived.

When McAfferty reshot the fleet the basker was still there, its dorsal fin curved gently over to one side, the great cruising bulk of it clearly visible just under the surface of the water. It crossed him again, so close that he could clearly see the long parallel rows of its open gills, rose pink against its darker flank. He wondered idly what it would take to kill such a creature. Beached and chain-sawed into freezer-sized chunks, it would keep him in bait for more than a month. The weak point of a fish, he knew, was not its heart or other vital organ, nor even its head, but the middle of its back. The back of this fish lay almost on the surface; watching it as it came three-quarters on to his bow once more, McAfferty, spurred perhaps in his diffident heart by the potential brag of it, had a rush of blood to the head. He threw open the morse control and heard the Lister chunter loud and fast as he aimed the heavy iron strapped keel of his boat just ahead of the place where the black triangle of the basker's dorsal fin cut water.

He got within maybe fifteen feet of it. From that distance he was forced to watch helplessly as it flicked its tail and glided languidly a fathom or so below his keel. When it resurfaced McAfferty imagined it was laughing at him. He cursed it, then cursed and laughed at himself for a fool.

Leaving the bay, he tucked in behind a ledge and picked up the dan-buoy marking the last fleet for which there was bait remaining. This took him from the smooth green elasticity of the backswell into an area of more broken water where the southwesterly began to drive at the corner. Here the sweep of the great basalt cliffs opened up a glimpse of a new stretch of coastline scattered about with skerries and sea-stacks, exposed to gales and too difficult and remote for the chancers. In this direction lay the best fishing of all, and the rest of his gear; the end of his reach was marked by a stack shaped like the head and shoulders of a human figure emerging from the sea holding a basket. If he could see the *cailleach* there was a good likelihood of fishing in that direction; if not, any wind with a bit of west in it was likely to be winning.

Today he could see her. But he had no bait. As he hauled the fleet he began mentally totting up. Between the poor lobster fishing and low crab prices there would be little, this week, to add to his nest-egg. For apart from his weekly half-dozen drams McAfferty lived frugally, and had been saving up. A bride-price. 'I've got a bit put by, now,' he would be able to say to a prospective betrothed. He was realistic enough to know what he had, and had not, to offer. The small croft, informally sublet but with a run-down garden maybe waiting for a tending hand, the house which he kept in good repair and tidy enough, more or less as he would keep a boat: these things were substantial, anyway. And himself? His hair was thinning, McAfferty knew, but almost uniquely among his peers he still had all his own teeth. 'Look, not even a filling,' he might say proudly one day, like a car salesman drawing attention to the bright chromed grillwork on one of his less-new models.

And finally there was the nest-egg, the modestly comfortable six thousand-plus pounds salted away safely in the Halifax. A refurbishing of the house, of course; that would help establish the marital protocols, too. Together with his prospective he would thumb through the pages of the Great Universal catalogue until they came to the bedroom furnishings. Here McAfferty would wait anxiously for her opinion on the matter of beds. Would she defer to him? You had, he concluded again, to be realistic.

If you had anyone. There was an English widow, a little eccentric but well enough disposed towards him. Could he propose to an incomer? The tangles would no longer matter if she accepted him. McAfferty shook his head at the empty creels. No fishing. No proper background. No wife. It was the fault of outsiders. It was the fault of the weather and the missed forecast. It was the fault of – but the second last creel came up just then, and McAfferty saw the conger.

It was a big one, probably the biggest he'd ever seen, a good four and a half feet long, maybe closer to five. As he watched it thrash about in the roomy parlour creel he was already appraising it. Cut crosswise into steaks it was worth thirty baits. That meant another two fleets. And in the matter of lobsters, who could say? Sometimes they came in a rush at the end to turn a bad day around, several, perhaps, in a single creel.

But first there was the matter of killing the creature. Of all the fish in the sea the conger had, McAfferty knew, the most tenacious grip on life with the ability to slither about for hours in the fish hold of a trawler. This gave it a mystique augmented by its serpent-like appearance. Secretly McAfferty feared the species just a little. Perhaps he had already killed too many, usually with the service of two good knives: one to pin his quarry briefly, then something big and heavy to lay across its spinal nerve. Something like the lost bait knife. He took out his three-inch pocket knife, the only blade he had now. Working that through the vital centre was, he knew, going to be quite a problem.

He opened the creel door and began stabbing ineffectively at the thrashing coils of the fish. It must have felt the surface wounds well enough, though, for all at once it gave a convulsive leap that folded the blade of the pocket knife in against the three lower fingers of McAfferty's right hand. He flinched at the sight of his own lacerated flesh, the start of his own blood, and swore for the shock of it. The conger, meantime, had hoisted itself on to the upper eye of the creel; from very close, it seemed, McAfferty saw its gaping mouth, the rows of minuscule but raspy-sharp teeth, the pale wrinkles of flesh under its powerful jaw, the bleak coldness of its fish's eye, and in real uncertainty, fuelled by his shock and pain, he recoiled from it. Catching his foot in a turn of the leader rope he lurched backwards into the well of the boat, bringing the opened parlour and a whole other mess of creels from the stack down on top of himself as he grabbed for support. The conger writhed in the tangled leader, lathering it into a blue froth of polypropylene. Suddenly it came right out of the ropes to lie across his lower abdomen.

Everything seemed to become still. McAfferty gave over from panicky flight to this stillness, feeling the muscular weight of the fish as it coiled on top of him. It was not all that much shorter than he, he'd lost his second knife and, as he lay there with it, the thought came to him that this was the most equal contest of the day. Perhaps he was a little out of his senses; whatever, to his mind it was now eycing his jugular, his windpipe.

Without taking his eyes from the conger he extended his free right arm and tried to ease the creels away from his legs. The fresh movement brought it to life again and it slithered forward and coiled right up against the prop of his left arm and came on to his upper chest and shoulder. He yelled then and tried to push it away, but he was hard jammed against the stack and there wasn't anywhere much to push it. It was inches from his face now, his nostrils were full of it, the rank, musky, disgusting conger stink. He pushed again, jamming it momentarily against a creel bar. Instantly he felt it begin to flex and slip out from under his grasp. He saw its back arch powerfully towards his face once more. In fear and loathing McAfferty fell back on to the only weapon left to him, that which made them as equals, and bit.

By luck, or perhaps by instinctive good aim, his teeth found two of the superficial wounds his knife had already made to either side of its spine. He clenched his jaws and the muscles of his neck as it thrashed about, trying to free itself. Pushing himself out from under the creels he felt for the pocket knife. Suddenly, though, the knife didn't seem to matter. McAfferty stood right up now, holding on to the hauler, and felt his teeth travel ever more deeply into the bunched dorsal muscles. Though his nostrils were swimming in the stench of it, the live flesh seemed oddly sweet in taste.

He felt the soft, cartilage-like bone of its spine. Perhaps, if anyone had been there to hear him, there might have been heard from McAfferty a muffled roar, then. Certainly there was a roaring sound in his head, a roaring against all of it, to all of it: his mother, his dead father, yes, his fellows, his lineage, his whole life, all the tangles and frustrations binding, but only half binding him to this soft-harsh fickle unrequiting land, and all the while the roaring was going on he felt the perfect teeth that would maybe never smile outward from the mock-gilt frame of a wedding photo travel onward, through the conger's spine, until abruptly its thrashings ceased.

He dropped it into the bait box, straightened his gear, hauled the last creel and reshot, before pausing to bind up his fingers with plasters from the first-aid box. Resting on the dan, then, he looked around. The lull in the wind, if it had been a lull, had been temporary; now it had freshened perceptibly, though bringing with it not the rain of the expected frontal trough but strong, bright sunshine. He could see the *cailleach* but the sun also picked out a heavy creaming of foam at the bows of the now returning ferry, as well as the white of its bridge. Behind, it played on a burn that tumbled down the black basalt, bursting in a little plume of spray and a tiny fragment of rainbow that gave the burn the likeness of a single gay thread in an otherwise endlessly severe bodice. To the south gannets were working the troughs, their streamlined bodies flashing white as they divebombed a passing shoal of small fry; nearer, the light glimmered also on the glassy, underwater-seeing orbs that were the eyes of a passing seal which had turned its head curiously towards him as it paused in its own foraging. But for McAfferty the hunt was over, the foam, the troughs, the updraught catching the burn all meant one thing only. It was too late.

The forecast would have told him. He looked down at the conger. It would keep for the morrow, but he didn't fancy its company now. He could always buy or borrow bait somewhere and its stink, which would worsen in death, had begun to bother him again. He picked it up and hoiked it indifferently over the side, not pausing to watch as it sank slowly down to disappear into the kelp like the lost bait knife. For already his hands were on the controls. McAfferty eased the wheel around and turned his boat towards home.

YER WEE HAPPY BUS . . .

Tom Rae

. . . purring past doon the Ruchill road looked rerr and cosy tae the hardly movin queue outside the post office gettin a bit shivery in the thin cotton and nylon stuff now that it was September and beginnin tae have a wee nip in the air. And because they were bored stupid and didny have weans or hangovers tae distract them some of the auld yins noticed a grumpy-lookin wummin the same age as themselves, auld enough for the registered state pension that is, lookin oot the bus windae at them, just above the pp bit in happy she was but out of sight even before somebody said, *Wid ye lookit the face oan that yin fur christ's sake* and the queue shuffled forward another wee bit. *Yer wee happy bus ma arse*, said somebody else.

But that just shows how ye never really know nothing cause the people oan the bus were saying the very same thing every one of them that got oan along the way that mornin; *Aw that's beyond a joke, driver, yer wee happy bus, whose idea wis that?* and the young driver called Travis, Susan asked his name, explained ten times over that the normal bus had broke doon that morning and what were they moaning aboot, this was a better bus any day.

And the grump wummin wisnae a grumpy wummin

either naw, she was just screwing up her nose because her glasses were slippin. They were too big for her, more Dennis Taylor than grumpy really and she was trying desperately tae see because she thought she recognized a person in that queue. To be fair she had been grumpy earlier because she'd been on the bus for nearly two hours now, ferried halfway round Strathclyde to the other side of the Campsies and everywhere just to get from Maryhill to Ruchill but somebody had to get on first, Travis had apologized, and when she recognized the Ruchill clock back there she smiled as she remembered the time she and Janet worked in that hospital after they left Stornoway. It was on the night shift one night when they brought Tyrone Power in. Really ill he was with TB the doctor told her but he was still a handsome man too and all the nurses carryin on about her having to give him a bed bath but he was a real gentleman and she was sorry when she heard he died soon after.

Anyway that was them all on the bus now and they were nearly there she was thinkin when the bus went and stopped again just after going under the canal bridge before Maryhill road.

The cable telly people were diggin up the pavements again; they were everywhere this year and their wee yellow digger was half blockin the road, only the cars on the other side were gettin through, but it wouldny be long.

Travis wound doon the windae to lean his elbow on it and catch some fresh air while they were waitin but right away auld Anne fae Fintry who was sitting on the left-hand side close behind the driver felt a draught . . .

Aye, daewit the auld wummin says, son, youse youngyins

don't feel the cauld like us, croaked a gravelly voice that was Susan's, backing up auld Anne.

Yer a right moaner so ye are, he answered but he was only kiddin on he was annoyed, you could tell he was ready for a bit banter.

Moaners ur we? A half an hour late and stuck in traffic oan yer wee happy bus . . .

Aye, and he drove us past aw they cemeteries, Susan, is that no ridiculous considerin eh? said Mima.

Susan fae Springburn was the last tae get oan every day so she didny know this but that didny matter, she was soon tellin them a story wi a cemetery in it.

Auld Anne who was nearly eighty-three, yes but she could still fight her own battles thank you very much, sat glarin ower as Susan rambled on . . .

Ma first man's buried in there in St Kentigern's, an industrial accident so it wis. Jim didny even get a penny cause he paid no heed to the safety procedures they said . . . bloody hellish.

Listen to her auld Anne was thinking, a voice like emery paper, she was just like those new neighbours lettin the cistern overflow, leak and flood the path for ten days last winter and always ready to tell you all their private business. And it was Lambhill protestants called that cemetery so she was right about that Susan woman in that department too.

Chrissy was watchin Anne starin at Susan who was still goin oan aboot Jim, only Mima beside her was startin tae talk aboot her man Roy who spent all his time in the garden . . . That look in auld Anne's eyes, the energy to take a scunner like that in her condition, my God, she hadn't learned anything in life thought Chrissy though she could see the annoying type Susan was. It had taken her years to get used to the Glasgow ways, they were all noise but not that bad, auld Anne was just a middle-class snob her son would say. Mima was still tellin her about Roy so she just nodded and said mhum now and again. Her daughter sometimes complained she could be really ignorant to people but that was the way she was. Mima wasn't bothered anyway she was the same herself, you just wanted to speak with another person sometimes instead of the wee dog or the wireless.

And she was glad she was beside a friendly soul like Mima who sat with her now every day rather than some of them. Look at that woman Liz who got on at Summerston and never spoke, she could just catch her in the corner of her eye two seats back, she would never see auld Anne's age: people with that yellow complexion never did. Tyrone Power was a bit that way when they brought him in.

Awright, there's the windae up if that'll please yese, Travis was saying.

Less of your cheek would please us, said Susan, *and get a move on.* The cabletelmen were wavin the bus through now . . . *and whit kinda name's that anywey . . . Travis . . . wis yer mammy a country and western fan, son?*

Haha, very funny, missus.

They were comin up to the lights now at Queen Margaret Drive. Chrissy turned round a bit as if she was lookin oot the windal but it was to get her good ear facing the two at the back . . . they were talkin about religion. She could only make out bits and pieces . . . *husband's a pastor and drives to Aberdeen every weekend . . . congregation there . . .* Which one was speaking? Those two were well off people with big cars Mima had told her, one of them was a teacher but they weren't allowed to drive back in them after it. The one with the long hair like a wee lassie would be the pastor's wife, she looked tired and dressed like the religious nuts back home in Stornoway. Chrissy never went there now but she could see her sister Norma with the long grey hair and ankle-length skirt just like that . . . *on cable* and *Lord providing new opportunities to reach his people,* the tired voice was sayin.

She was aware that Mima had stopped speakin all of a sudden. There was a wasp oan the bus. It was buzzin like mad and attackin the windal pane above Mima's heid. You just had to ignore them and they flew away was Chrissy's attitude, they would all be dead soon, but the Susan wan was turned right round, the terror in her eyes you would have thought she was facin up to a murderer.

Ah hate they things, we've been plagued wi the buggers this summer, who's got a paper?

Chrissy was sure then that Susan had a wig on too because when Susan was reachin for the *Daily Record* stuck in behind the driver's seat she was careful how she moved her head that cautious way.

But while Susan was still foldin up the paper Chrissy saw the blue jacket of a man's arm reachin across herself and Mima, the palm spread out . . . a man's smell . . . then the bus lurched and he nearly missed it but the second time you could hear the breakin noise of the wasp squashed against the glass. The man made sure it didny drop oan them keepin it tight in his fist as he went back tae his seat.

Liz wais the only wan that saw him drop it just before he sat down then stub it intae the floor like a dout.

He was the only man that got picked up, why was it
it was mainly all women Chrissy was thinkin . . .

That poor man, Mima was whisperin, *he's from near*
Inverness somewhere and has to stay with his sister down here
for the month, that must make it harder. Ah was talkin to
him yesterday on the way back after you got off, Chrissy, Ah
didny catch his name, Alastair Ah think, he was very quiet,
missin his friends Ah think.

He looked quiet. Chrissy found herself thinkin about
how hard his hands were to just grind up a wasp like
that just like her own man's used to be when he was in
the brickworks. He had to clean the grease off them
with Swarfega every night and they always used to joke
about how rough his hands were in bed . . . it took two
years after he retired till all the hacks and dirtiness
disappeared. That man must still be workin, not long
till he would be ready to retire but . . . shame.

They were halfway doon Byres road now and Susan
was still givin it to the driver about lettin the wasp in.
If it had stung one of them in their condition it could
have had serious consequences she warned him like a
legal expert.

A tired sun was strugglin up there in the overcast sky.
The weatherman had got it wrong, those spits of rain
earlier weren't goin to come to anythin. A young couple
rushed out the Burger King eatin burgers, students
probably, they had that Oxfam look. For a laugh they
were takin a bite of each other's burger. That made
Chrissy a bit queasy to think of the greasy meat but the
fact that there would always be young couples doin that
sort of daft thing cheered her up.

And there was no more stoppin yer wee happy bus,
the next traffic lights were green, *Fuckit*, said the young

guy in the white Astra comin doon Highburgh Road half plannin tae jump the lights, now brakin hard, *Whit ur ye lookin at ye auld cunt?* as Chrissy sailed past looking doon at him.

Left into Church Street then left again on to Dumbarton Road there was the Art Galleries they used to take the weans into before the carnival in the Kelvin Hall at Christmas cause they never had the money for the rides, the weans never knew, they liked the museum as much as the carnival; maybe not Mhairi, it was the stuffed animals that did that but you had to drag Kenneth away from the dinosaurs and the armour suits when he was a boy . . .

All the ambulances lined up outside casualty made it hard for the bus to turn but Travis eventually managed it with one of the gatemen helpin (more like slaggin his drivin really). The bloke finished the coffee he was drinkin and threw the polystyrene cup on to a flowerbed then yanked on the waistband of his trousers, it was obvious the uniform was too wee for him.

Right youse lot, wur here, shouted Travis as the bus doors whooshed open, *mind the step.* Auld Anne was already on her feet usin the back of the seat in front tae edge oot. *Wait oan hen and Ah'll gie ye a haun aff,* shouted Mima stuffin the pink card back into her handbag, she was neurotic about the appointment times. *C'moan, Chrissy, wur here, this is the Beatson,* she said but she was already gettin up tae help auld Anne.

Chrissy sat where she was lookin down at the flowers. They looked even more orange than before. Nasturtiums. Maybe it was last night's rain had made the leaves greener after the heatwave all summer, plants needed to drink too . . .

The gateman who'd been drinkin the coffee looked along the bus and saw a grumpy woman wi ginormous specs staring at the polystyrene cup he'd tossed into the flowers . . . right enough he shouldny have done it but you would think the folk that came here would have more to worry about than a wee plastic cup fur fuck's sake, he was thinkin . . .

But it was herself Chrissy was annoyed with . . . six weeks ago after her first treatment getting into the car with Kenneth and Mhairi just here beside these orange flowers . . . they were so beautiful that day those flowers. She wasn't think just talkin out loud when she heard her own voice far away sayin, *You know, you don't realize how attached you get to the things in this world* and as soon as she said it she could have bitten her tongue off. That was the reason why she looked grumpy right now, that and remembering how quiet the car was when they drove home that day, nobody spoke, she'd upset them that much with her stupid mouth, she could still feel the pain of her grown-up children trying not to let the tears burst . . .

Chrissy . . . C'moan, hen, snap ooty it, time tae get aff.

That was Susan talkin to her and takin her by the arm as if she needed a help up, she just let her, still jabbering on in that gravelly voice of hers. You could tell she was terrified of bein on her own for a minute, she was a poor soul really. *Chrissy,* she was saying, *ye know the bit Ah hate the worst? Don't laugh noo . . . it's jist efter they stick the needle in, Ah don't know why, but ma arse gets that itchy, Ah want tae scream so Ah dae, whit aboot you? Dis your arse get itchy? Whit kinda cocktail is it they must be pumpin intae us eh?*

Just a bag of nerves, Chrissy thought as they stepped

down off the bus, she probably blabbed on like that in
front of her family. Some people didn't think, that was
the trouble.

SASKATCHEWAN

Lorn Macintyre

It's Games Day. The sun has risen over the bay and is coming through my cotton curtains, laying a golden quilt on my bed. I hear Father crossing the landing, then the rasp of his razor as he shaves, singing a Gaelic song. He is secretary of the Games and he knows that everything is ready on the field above the town. The marquees that came on the cargo boat have been erected; the latrines dug. He rinses his razor under the tap and I hear the Old Spice I gave him for his Christmas being slapped on. Mother is now up, going down to the kitchen.

I go to the corner of my bedroom and lift up the two swords. They have authentic looking hilts, but the blades are made of silver-painted wood. I cross them on the carpet and lace up my pumps. Today I am dancing at the Games, and this year I hope to win the sword dance. I have been practising all winter, making the floor of my bedroom vibrate, with Mother claiming that the ceiling in the sitting-room will come down on top of her as she watches a soap on our temperamental set which sometimes has to be slapped to restore the signal. But Father came up to watch me dancing, sitting on the bed as I danced by the window over my dud swords.

'I'll be amazed if you don't win it this year, Marsali.'

It's Games morning and I'm practising, landing on my toes as softly as possible to save them for the competition. Soon Mother will call up that breakfast is ready, but I will eat nothing more than a brown egg because I have seen competitors in previous years throwing up behind the marquee.

I know where Father is. He is at the sitting-room window, watching for the dark blue bow of the steamer to slide up to the pier. It left one of the islands in the dawn and is packed with spectators for the Games. Many of them are Father's customers in the bank, but that isn't why I hear the door closing as he goes down to the pier to wait by the gangway. It's for the pleasure of hearing the Gaelic of another island spoken. I have put my swords away and can see the first of the spectators coming along the street from my high window. The men have raincoats folded over their shoulders and caps pushed to the backs of their heads as they look into the window of Black the ironmonger's. Their stout wives are at the other window where knitting needles are crossed in balls of wool.

The procession up to the field musters at the memorial clock and is led by the laird with a plaid over his shoulder and a long stick. The pipe band behind him is followed by the spectators, going up past the aromatic wild roses on the back brae. But I am already on the field, my number pinned to my frilled blouse. I have on my pumps and am practising in the subdued coolness of the tent, using my swords. Mothers are fussing round other competitors, straightening the pleats of kilts and exhorting them to dance as well as they can.

A girl comes in. She is pretty, with a blue velvet bonnet angled on her blonde hair, and a plaid, held at her shoulder by a cairngorm brooch, trailing at her heels. She is carrying a holdall that says Canadian Pacific, and in her other hand she has two large swords.

'Hi,' she says to us all, and comes across to the corner of the tent where I am exercising to make my toes supple. 'I'm Jeannie Maclean.'

I go into my bag and check the programme. There is no such name down for the sword dance. She sees me looking at her quizzically and she says: 'I'm a late entry. Mom posted the form a month ago but it never reached here. I went to see the secretary and he says I can compete since I've come such a long way.'

'Where are you from?' I ask.

'Saskatchewan.'

Immediately that name takes on a romantic resonance and I want her to say it again.

'It's in Canada,' she informs me, lacing up her pumps. 'We have wheat fields that go on for miles.'

I am trying to imagine the ripe golden crop waving in the breeze when she adds more information. 'Our people came from this island.'

'From here?' I say, surprised.

'U-huh. They were cleared last century and they found their way to Saskatchewan. They did pretty well. We have four combine harvesters on our farm and my father has a herd of Aberdeen Angus he shipped across.' It's not a boast but a factual statement.

'Are these real swords?' I enquire, reaching across to touch them.

'Claymores. My folks brought them across from this island. My grandfather said we fought with them at Culloden.'

'If they came from here they must have spoken Gaelic,' I say.

'Sure, but we lost it when we intermarried. My great-grandmother was a squaw. I'd love to learn Gaelic.' (She pronounces it Gale-ick.) 'Do you speak it?'

I nod, but I'm getting too involved in this conversation instead of preparing for the competition. She, after all, is a rival, and as she lays the swords on the turf and begins a practice dance, I see how good she is. She's dancing as she converses with me, her shadow turning on the canvas wall of the tent. 'I've been doing this since I was three, first with two wooden spoons on the floor of the kitchen. I need to win today. Mom's outside.'

I don't want to stay in the tent to watch her practise because it's undermining my confidence, so I go over the hill, past the latrines, already busy with early drinkers, to a quiet hollow where I lay down my swords in the hum of insects and make my own music with my mouth to dance to. But I feel there is something lacking. My feet are heavy and I am aware of the clumsiness of my hands above my head. As I turn my foot touches a blade, and I stop, upset.

I hear Father's voice through the megaphone calling the competitors for the sword dance. As I go back over the hill I feel he has betrayed me by letting the girl from Saskatchewan – I am beginning to hate the name – enter for the competition when the rule says entries in advance. The dancing judges from the mainland are sitting in the shade of a lean-to beside the platform, with paper to mark the competitors on the card tables above their knees. I sit on the hill to watch, but I am not impressed by the standard.

'Number 79, Jeannie Maclean.'

She comes up on to the platform with her swords under her arm and there is a confab among the judges. Yes, she can use her own swords, as long as the steward lays them down. He makes them into a cross for her on the boards. She puts her hands on her hips and bows to the judges as the pipes tune up. I see from the first steps what a beautiful dancer she is. I am watching her toes and they hardly seem to touch the boards, springing in the air above the blades, now touching a diced stocking. The people around me on the hillside are enthralled. To my left there is a woman also wearing a Maclean kilt, with a cape. She is standing, holding up her thumbs to her dancing daughter.

Jeannie Maclean is turning in the air, her kilt swirling. She is twenty seconds off the trophy which is waiting in a table in the secretary's tent. Four nights ago I watched father polishing it, and he told me: 'Your name will be on this, Marsali.'

Jeannie Maclean is performing her last movement when she comes down, heavily. I see the side of the pump touch the blade which slices through the leather. She is lying on the boards, holding her bleeding foot, and her mother is shouting behind me instead of going down to her injured daughter. 'You damn fool!'

Father calls for Dr MacDiarmid through the megaphone and he comes in his Bermuda shorts with his medical bag. Jeannie Maclean is helped off the platform and hops to the first-aid tent, her hand on the doctor's shoulder, to have her foot stitched.

It's my turn to dance and I turn to bow to the judges in the lean-to. How dearly now do I wish that the trophy for the sword dance was going across the ocean to

Canada, to sit in a glass case in a prairie house where Gaelic was once spoken. But Jeannie Maclean is out of the competition. As my toes touch the boards I am dancing to the refrain: Sas-katch-ew-an, Sas-katch-ew-an. I see Father crossing the field, his secretary's rosette on his lapel. He has come to watch me and he stands, smiling in encouragement. I know I have never danced better because this is a performance for him. Sas-katch-ew-an, Sas-katch-ew-an. I am reaching for the sky. Mother is on the hillside waving but she has never really been interested in Highland Dancing or Gaelic because she's from the mainland.

I can feel my toes so sure, as they come down between the blades. I turn to face my father, my knuckles on my hips. This is for you, Father, for all the patience and love, for the Gaelic words you give me. I turn to face the marquee. I can see a slumped shadow on the canvas, another shadow hanging over it, an arm raised. This is for you, Jeannie Maclean, with your wounded foot, your treacherous swords and your angry mom. I have nothing but pity and love, and as I bow to the judges and the applause rises I know that one day I will go to Saskatchewan.

THE DINNER PARTY

Moira Forsyth

.

I dinna care. I says to her, stuff your job, I'll easy get anither een. Winna be sae easy for you tae get somebody else to clean up efter you. There's nae mony wid dee it – God, fit a sotter the kitchen wis aye in when I went in in the mornin. Dishes a ower the place – the hale a yesterday's never mind breakfast. Cornflakes in the sink, half a loaf left oot on the table, the cooker caked wi grease, somethin sticky spilt on the flair . . . and that wis on the good days.

I'd been deein it for mair than six months – cleanin up their leavins. At first, I jist set to, rowin up my sleeves, nae mindin. Other folk's sotter is never as bad as your ain. Nae that my hoose ever looked like theirs – God forbid. I like things tidy, and nane a my bairns wid ha dared dump fitba buits caked wi mud in *my* lobby on a fawn carpet. As I say, I didna mind a that – she paid me well enough. Fifty pee an hour over the goin rate and a tenner extra at Christmas. They werena short a money – you widna hae to be, livin in that street, in a hoose that size. Fairly splashed it aroon and a – she hid new claes near every week and the bairns had computers and hi-fis up to the ceilin in their bedrooms.

But they were a funny pair. It took me a while tae click on – I dinna ken, maybe I'm a bittie slow. Thocht

they'd somebody bidin . . . Then I realized it wisna that
– they hid separate bedrooms, him and her . . . Hers
peach and pale blue, claes awey, underwear left on the
flair, glossy magazines, bottles a perfume – place smelt
like Debenhams make-up counter on a Setterday mornin fan the lassies spray testers on ilka body that gings
by, and the air's thick wi it.

But he didna sleep there. His wis the other big bedroom at the top a the stairs. Books lyin aboot in heaps,
a red and black downie and a black carpet showed every
bit a fluff – some job tae hoover, believe you me. And
bottles a fancy aftershave – room reeked a that and his
French cigarettes in a big blue box he'd brocht back
duty free. He wis often awa abroad. So what wi her
perfume and his smokin, I aye opened the windas when
I went in tae clean.

When I telt my chum Lorna aboot the separate bedrooms she said it wis jist like the aristocracy.

'The Queen and Prince Philip,' she says, 'ken, *they*
dinna sleep in the same room. Disna mean there's nae
hanky panky.'

'Fit, the *Queen*?' I says to her. 'Getting on a bit for
that sort a thing, is she nae?' Made me uncomfortable,
thinkin aboot it. Ye canna even imagine the Queen wi
her claes aff, never mind . . . anyhow, Lorna tells me
tae look at the pillows.

'Ye'll easy ken if there's been mair than een body in
the bed.'

'O aye,' I says, 'maybe so, but she strips the beds
Monday mornin afore I get there. Then I make them
up fresh.'

I decided it wis nee a my business. I stopped sayin
anythin to Lorna, she wis gaun ower the score, I thocht,

like some kinda peepin Tom. I did wonder though. They wis perfectly friendly, ken fit I mean? And the bairns nice-mannered – well, nae to each other a course. They wis teenagers. But OK wi me. I only sa them in the holidays – my mornins wis Monday, Wednesday and Friday.

No, it wisna that, or the state a the hoose, that scunnered me. Min, cleanin the bathrooms wis nae joke – three of them, would you believe? Made me glad we'd only the one, though there had been times afore Karen left home we hid tae cross oor legs and hope for the best. Hours, she spent in there. No, fit finished me with the Lawrences wis the dinner perty. I'll never forget it, lang as I live.

'We're having some people to dinner on Friday,' she says to me, settin doon her briefcase and comin intae the kitchen. She's nae usually hame in the middle a the day, and I wondered at first if she wisna weel. But she looked as bonny as ever in her dark red suit, the skirt a bittic on the short side, I would say, for somebody her age, but never mind, she's got the figure for it. She looked the picture a health wi her hair black and glossy swingin forward and her make-up fresh and her rings flashin.

'I just wondered,' she says, 'I hope it's not an imposition – would you be free to help out?'

'Oh no,' I says, 'my Billy's very fond of me, but even he widna ca me a cook.' She laughed.

'Oh, the food's all taken care of. But I could do with someone to hand things round, stack the dishwasher . . . clear up afterwards. I'd pay you, of course.'

'Oh, of course,' I says, but she misses the sarcasm, just smiles at me.

'*Would* you, Betty? Do be an angel and say yes.'

'Oh aye.' I says. 'I'll have to check wi Billy. But I'm sure that'll be all right. What time would you like me to come?'

Really, I was quite looking forward to it. Billy's darts night is Friday, and since the Catherine Cookson story finished there's been nothin on the TV on a Friday night I've fancied. And I was curious to see their friends, and fit kind a food she would have. Tell you the truth, I've aye fancied haein a dinner perty mysel.

'Why don't ye then?' Billy says, when I telt him aboot it.

'My cookin, mainly,' I tells him, and we laugh.

'We could buy stuff,' he suggests. 'Marks and Spencer – that's fit Rosie does.' Rosie's his sister – works full-time in an insurance office, so that's her excuse.

'Ach,' I says, 'folk like us dinna hae dinner perties.'

'Well, I dinna ken,' he shaks his heid, 'fan the bairns wis at hame ye were never done feedin other folk.'

'That's different,' I says.

But still, the idea kinda lodged in my mind. And on the Friday night when I saw her lang polished table wi the candles lit in the tall silver and blue candlesticks, and the crystal glasses sparklin and the cutlery a laid oot – God kens fit they needed a thon forks for – somethin tugged at ma hert, and for a minute I wished I wis well-aff, earnin guid money in some office wi computers an big desks and fluorescent licht and cheese plants . . . Then I gied mysel a shak, and set to tae help her in the kitchen.

'Your table's very bonny,' I says.

'That's the easy bit,' she smiles, and gies me the plates for the starter. White plates wi a red and bold border.

'My grandmother's – Coalport. We don't often use them. Too precious.'   ·

The starter was smoked salmon and wee bits a salad stuff and thin broon bread.

'Nice and simple,' she says.

Nice and expensive, I thinks, but there you are, money was nae object.

She had artichoke soup, and duck breasts stuffed with apricots and I dinna ken fit, and wee green pea pods and new tatties and mair . . . nae Marks and Sparks ready meals here, I could see that. She was in aul leggins and a baggy T-shirt, dartin here and there. She'd taen the day aff, been at it since mornin.

'Where's the bairns?' I asked, kennin they were usually around when food as on the go.

'Out,' she says. 'Phil's mother's.'

She left me to tidy while she went to get dressed up. Kitchen was bad, richt enough, but I've seen it worse. And the rest of the hoose was immaculate – her and me, we'd spent the mornin getting the hale place into shape. She telt me then that the folk she had comin was a to dee wi his work. He wis wi an oil compnay. Ye see fok wi sillar in Aiberdeen, ye can be sure they work in a big concrete block aff Anderson Drive wi a stone plinth in the driveway and some word carved into it that ends in -oco or -aco, and sounds American.

'Do you know them, then?' I asked, feelin sorry for her, gaun to a this trouble for oil executives and their wives.

'Oh yes. I play squash with Helen – she's Phil's immediate boss. And Sheila and Don are old friends. I don't know Kate so well – she's from the States, terribly deep South, you know? But Gavin, her partner, he's

Glaswegian – such a hoot – he and Phil go back a long way.'

I revised my ideas: it sounded as if the women were the oil executives. I set oot the smoked salmon, imagined them a sittin there wi their glasses a wine, talking business.

She came down wi a black dress showin a lot top and bottom, if you get my meanin. Low in the neck and short in the skirt. But she looked very classy, and her earrings and the collar thing she hid on were silver – heavy modern stuff. I took good note – my Karen, she was aye interested in the details. Karen works in Fraser's, training to be a buyer. Nae that Sara Lawrence ever looks near Fraser's. By the look, a her jewellery's fae Princes Street, or maybe London. He had a dinner jacket on, came in and thanked me for helpin, and set out a row of bottles of red wine alongside the radiator.

'That should warm them up nicely,' he says, winkin at me. I had the feeling he's had a wee dram a'ready, ken fit I mean?

I hadna even thocht aboot it, been ower busy, but when I heard the voices in the hall, I could smell abeen the duck cookin, great wafts a expensive scent and aftershave, and my knees went a to jelly. I had to sit doon. Fit it wis, I was terrified I'd drop somethin, mak a feel a mysel, ruin their evenin.

They were in the sittin room for ages, drinkin and laughin. Then she comes in and says, 'We're going in to have the smoked salmon now – put the soup on low, Betty, and stoke up the drawing-room fire, would you? I'll come through when we need you,'

The sittin room smelt sweet, and the tang a whisky was there and a, ahint the perfume and the wood-smoke. I put on a coupla logs, and stacked the glasses on a tray. Then I saw the stopper of the whisky decanter hidna been put on right, so I went to sort it. It occurred to me than a wee bit Dutch courage widna ging amiss.

Then I cerried the glasses into the kitchen and started ladlin the soup into the big china tureen. Serve it at the table, she'd said, and I could see the sense a that.

It went fine – the hale dinner. I hid a wee nip in atween each course and that helped. It wis a sae bonny – the wine rich and dark red in the glasses, the pink flowers in the centre, the women in their lovely frocks and diamonds sparklin, and the men in their dickeys and bow ties. Just like the films. I was fair teen on wi it a, storin it up tae tell Karen and Billy. I suppose I was feelin well warmed by the time they had their puddin, so I wisna a that conscious a the wey things were gaun in the dinin room. Every now and then he comes through for another bottle a wine, richt enough, an they wis very merry. But it wis a perty, and ye're entitled to a bit jollity at a perty.

And then, I dinna ken, somethin changed. They sat a lang time wi their coffee and Belgian chocolates. I sat in the kitchen and ate the rest a the chocolate mousse, though it hid rather too much alcohol in it for my taste. I kent I should mak a start on the dishes, but I was gey weary. So I put my feet up on a kitchen chair, and ate a few a the oatcakes they'd hid wi their soup, an some cheese . . . an one or two caul tatties. I'd hid nae dinner, ye ken, and whisky aye gies me an appetite. Then I got to my feet and started to clear up. But I nearly dropped a plate, and since the Coalport couldna ging in the dishwasher, I hid to dee it a by hand. . . . I got a fleg when the plate nearly went on the flair – decided to leave the washin up till I felt mair like mysel.

But I didna. In fact, I was affa queasy. At my age, right enough, I shoulda kent better. Blame the whisky. I went to the toilet aff the hall, but somebody musta been in, so I nipped upstairs and into the big bathroom on the first landing. After a while, somebody came and tried the door, but the state I was in I couldna even cry oot *jist a minute!* But ye're aye better when ye've got rid a fit wis makin ye feel sick. I washed my face, but I wis still a bittie fushionless, so I sat doon on the flair, leaning on the wa. A of a sudden, I was sae tired I could hardly keep my een open. Maybe I even dozed off a wee filey. Nae lang, I couldna afford that – there was still a thon dishes to get through. God.

When I cam oot a the bathroom, the hoose was silent. I stood and listened, but heard nothin ava. Then, from his bedroom right next to me, I heard gigglin. Lorna was richt, I thocht, and I've been in there sae lang a'body's gone hame and the two a them's in his bed . . . The door was wide open, so I could hear them plain enough, and it's nae the kinda noise you could mistak for anythin else. I went downstairs, thinkin I'd shut the kitchen door and quietly clean up, then ring for my taxi. She gien me mony for a taxi. Then, as I got to the bottom of the stairs, I heard the same sounds. From the sittin room. I couldna help mysel – I went right up to the doorway. It was open, and although I couldna see anybody, I heard them. Then I saw somethin. Lyin on the flair, crumpled like she'd pud it aff in a hurry, was her black dress, and next to it, the silver collar she'd been wearin.

I stepped back, turning by instinct to the dinin room.

It was empty, at least, but my God ... Later, I says to Billy, and this is true, min, I dinna care fit they get up tae as far as their sex lives in concerned – that's neen a my business. But if ye'd seen thon bonny table – the sotter they'd left it in, the glasses tummled ower and the red wine makin a white mark on the lovely mahogany, and drippin on the carpet and the food *wasted* ... what they left on their plates wid feed us for a week.

'Dinna exaggerate,' he said, 'ye're just jealous. Never mind – you can hae yer ain dinner perty now. Ye'll ken a the ins and oots.'

He's laughin at me, ken, but I sat up in bed, my temper gettin the better a me.

'You micht think it's a joke, but if you think I'm slavin ower a hot stove so you and Annie Cairns can hump awa in my bed –'

'Ye dinna fancy Jimmy then?'

'Ach,' I says, 'be serious.'

I wis nearly sleepin when Billy says, 'Min, when Colis wis at the college, he had this book he wis reading and he read the first line and I thocht at the time it was a bit *ordinary*, like, for a famous book.'

'Fit? Billy, I wis jist aboot awa there – I'm *exhausted*. Fit?'

'This book, it started like this ...'

'Like what?'

'"The rich are different from you and me." '

'God's sake, Billy,' I says, 'if you hidna grasped that by now –'

'No,' he says. 'I canna say I hid. But now – well, there you are. You've proved it to me.' He laughed.

'Fit is't now?

'Thank God we're poor, Betty, eh?'

'It's a richt for you,' I says, 'I have to go back there Monday mornin.'

And I did. I kent somethin wis wrong seen as I opened the front door. She cam into the hall, dressed for work.

'There you are, Betty,' she says, very cool-like. 'I was waiting to see you.'

'Oh aye.' She flushed up a bit, didna look me in the eye.

'Betty,' she says, 'this isn't easy for me – you've been such a treasure . . . but on Friday night – were you unwell or something? You'd only to say.'

Tell the truth, I'd forgotten a aboot bein sick. It came back to me now, and I wondered if maybe she'd noticed I'd been at the whisky. I began to be feared I'd made a feel a mysel in front a them a. But I wisna sure, couldna really min much aboot servin up the dinner. And when you're nae sure of your ground, you're aye better to keep mum. So I did.

'The thing is,' she goes on, 'you simply abandoned everything – dishes, left-over food, the lot. I couldn't believe the mess on Saturday morning. I mean, the arrangement was that you'd *clear up*.'

My God, I thocht, the cheek of her, gettin worked up aboot a few dishes when she wis haein it awa wi some other woman's husband in the next room!

'I was sick,' I says. 'Something disagreed with me.'

'Oh.' She stood there, fiddlin with her rings. 'Well, I suppose – but Betty, you must realize – it was simply awful to come down to that . . . mess in the morning.'

That's when I lost it, got carried away. *You can stuff your job then, if that's how you feel. I can easy get anither een.*

And I did. I've a nice wee number servin school

dinners in the primary doon the road. There's a vacancy for a cook comin up shortly, and Billy says I should apply. School dinners – all in all, that's probably mair my line than dinner perties.

GIRL FROM THE NORTH COUNTRY

Andrew Greig

The old drove road curled over the shoulder of the hill like smoke from an old man's pipe, and down it that day a young man drove signing 'In Scarlet town, where I was born . . .' The wind was strong and the sound of his song arrived long before he did. Tyres crunched, the handbrake squeaked, a dog barked in the back of his father's Land-Rover. Clunk of the door, his boots scuffing the dirt. I stood up from behind the dyke.

His right hand went up inside his Barbour as though to protect his wallet or his heart. I smiled and put my hands down on the gate between us. He blushed then, he took a redder like a laddie while yellow hair blew over his face in the sharp wind. His jacket was the dun drab of the muir, and he was young and unsure for all his standing and southron education. I hooked my thumbs in the belt loops of my jeans and completed his song. 'Her name was Barbara Allen.'

My voice was sure and I sang it steadily for all that my heart was tossing with the corbies in the high trees about the heuch. I finished and his hair blew back and his eyes were paler than the cold March sky above us. He smiled his long-mouthed Elliot smile as his hand came down to the bolt of the gate, and I cursed the old grip that made me dip my head to him. I saw the grey-green lichen gripped to the wood, the blood-red stone clasped in his ring.

I slipped the bolt.

'Come by,' I said, and opened the gate wide.

'I'm sorry,' he said, 'do I know you?'

I stared him back.

'Why would you?'

'But you're from these parts?'

'I've been away a long time.'

The dog jumped out the back. He grabbed its collar and hung on as it snarled and slavered. The collar was finished with silver and on it his father's crest. The pride of it could make you laugh or greet. The hand that twisted the collar was pale, long-fingered, young. His arm was trembling from the strain or the wind.

'What brings you here?' he asked.

'Work. Yourself?'

He started dragging the hound back to the Land-Rover but never took his eyes off me.

'"Pleasure,' he said. 'Sport.' He nodded and I saw the rods and the gun behind the windscreen. 'Mid-term break.'

He threw the dog inside but still he hesitated.

'If you're in no hurry,' I said, 'there's time for all the kenning in the world.'

He blushed then jumped in and drove through to my side of the old dyke and the world fell like an apple into my hand.

I put the gate near to as he jumped down and his hound circled us. I smiled and came up to him yet still the boy hesitated with the car keys in his fist. In the trees about the dark heuch corbies skirled as a hawk flew overhead.

He glanced at his watch and laughed.

'And I thought home was dull,' he said. 'It seems the world's still young and full of surprises.'

I slipped my hand through the buttons of my coat.

'You are young. The world is as it's always been.' I laughed to take the edge off it, and came nearer him. 'The Border has aye been wild country.'

'The Border's been settled these three hundred years.'

He looked me up and down. His eyes flicked to the bracken where I'd lain waiting, then down my open coat and shirt. The hound bared its teeth and gurled but kept its distance.

'There's some have wildness yet,' I said, and unbuttoned.

He had his father's mouth, but young and sweet. I matched my lips to his as I had tried to match my tongue to his modern speech that he might better understand me. Chill hands were on my breasts, he held them as though they were something wonderful. He was full of juice, that boy. I could lift the ripeness of the world to my teeth and crunch.

I pushed him back.

'Send your hound hame,' I said. 'I'll not lie whiles he is here.'

He knelt and whispered in its ear, gave it a light skelp and the dog slipped under the gate and ran on towards the big house in the distant wood across the gorge. The hawk was still tummelin with the corbies in the trees as I took the keys from his hand.

He threw down his Barbour on the bracken, gallant that he was. The wallet fell half-out. His gutting knife winked at his hip.

'I want no metal blade in me,' I told him.

He laughed and tossed the knife into the bracken roots and I came down to him. This time he was more sure. Certainly he had been with the woman who was prepared for him, the tall one with fair hair pulled high on her white neck. But his touch was full of curiosity and wonder yet, and I doubted if there had been others, though his father had been with more than one too many.

With eyes closed there was no-time with the cool wind riding abune the muir and through our open clothes. The world was young as in the early days. We were not gripped save by each other.

I opened my eyes. The sun was in his golden hair. In its parting ripe fields unfolded to horsemen in ambush. In its blowing, men birled and fell. In its reddish roots I saw the burning farm, the cattle reived, the mother bled and herried.

The world was as it always was. I stopped his hand under my jeans.

'Tell me of your travels,' I said.

His chill fingers poised at the lip of my warmth, withdrew.

'Tell me about Italy.'

He stared up at me and I liked fine to twitch and guide him. He was young and biddable for all his Elliot pride, for all that he had sat in the big car at his father's side and watched him do his business on both sides of the Border. He was a youth who caught young could turn out well, and I had him in my clasp sure as the little claws that held the blood-red stone of his family ring.

I sat up.

'Tell me about Rome,' I said.

He sniffed his fingers doubtfully.

'What do you know of that?'

'It's common talk both sides of the Border,' I said and took his hand. 'Folk will aye talk about the doings of the likes of you.'

He was pleased with that and flashed his teeth. We lay close in the bracken bed while he told me of Rome and the Pope, of traffic, cafés and cardinals and the Italian women, and as I gently sucked his ring he told me of his father's penances.

'His sin must have been byordinar to need such penances?'

He looked away, towards the trees about the heuch where the river ran so deep, then to the rough pasture of the Border.

'Byordinar,' he said softly. 'That's an old word.'

'And an old sin?'

He twisted his fingers among the bracken roots.

'He was found not guilty and he is truly contrite. He's not the same man.'

Truly. Old Elliot sat in his castle jumping at shadows, starting at every passing car in the dale. He no longer drove, drunk nor sober, and he never went down Langholm way nor cast his eye at quines, and he paid his blood money into a dead woman's account on the fifth of every month.

'May he have rue time yet,' I said, then leaned over him and grazed upon him and we heard no more of Langholm or Rome. Only when I silently unbuckled his watch did he pull back and stare at me.

'I still can't place you,' he said.

I laughed down at him.

'You're from over the river?'

I sang 'In Scarlet town, where I was born', then laid myself upon him in earnest and he jumped like a colt as I unclipped my mother's brooch that held whatever modesty I possessed, and then there was no more to be said but the doing of it.

He pulled his breeks about him as I picked up his keys again. The fob was fashioned from a pierced gold coin, very old and worn. I held it sideways to the low sun to better see the pattern. That raised bump could be a man's head, or a hawk.

He yawned and frowned.

'I have a girlfriend,' he said, and put the knife back in his belt.

'Fiancée,' I said. 'I expect she's waiting for you.'

The ridge below the bump could be a dyke or a high collar. Certainly there were marks like undergrowth, and belike something half hidden among them. He frowned and had the grace to look shame-faced.

'And so docs my father.'

With very old worn things it is hard to be sure and easy to see what you may want to there. I sat up and pulled my coat about me.

'My faither does not,' I said. 'Nor does my mither.' I stood up and held my hand out. 'Walk with me across the brig and then I'll go my way.'

He sighed, but he had as little choice as I in any of these matters. His hause-bane rose and fell as he pulled the shirt on, his skin so white and goose-pimpled in the low sun.

'Don't worry,' I said. 'There'll be no tittle-tattle from me, and there'll be no bairn.'

The frown went but still he stared.

'Barbara Allen,' he murmured. 'This is the strangest day I've known.'

Sweet Jesu, he was gleikit, soft and dazed as men are after love. As love it might have been.

He leads the way on to the arching brig across the cleuch. I follow, looking down. Here it is dim and sheltered from wind and sight. At the far side we must go our ways. I call on him twice before he hears me above the thundering fall. I say the narrow brig with its low parpen, the drop below and the grey water sliding past, all make me light-headed. I must bide a moment.

He laughs but stops and comes back to me. The heuch above us overhangs, its underside dark with slabberin moss. I see myself fall with the water and stramash into the rocks below. He takes my arm.

'You're white-like,' he says. 'Don't look down.'

I nod and look past him to the far side of the brig. My heart is thunnerin.

'Was yon a kingfisher doun there?'

'Where?'

'Where the moss stops. I canna look. Tell me if you spy him.'

He leans and keeks over the edge. The brooch is slippy in my fingers.

'No.'

He turns quickly away, shrugs. He's impatient now, in a hurry to be gone. It will be late, and dark when he gets hame and his father waiting and his lady. He walks on past the middle of the brig.

'Wait for me,' I shout. 'I'm feart.'

He stops, turns round half smiling.

'Down there,' I whisper in his ear. 'Look again.'

He sighs and looks down again.

His body falls turning through the gloom, into the grey falls without a sound above their gowling.

The drove road is empty. Mirk seeps about the howes and mist is poosking from the river. I retrieve the coin from the fob and throw the keys away. I get into the Land-Rover and fumble till the brake's away then grunt and sweat till the muckle thing lurches across the brae, hesitates on the lip then disappears into the deep.

Long will his lady pine and long may Andrew Elliot wait for his only son and heir to come riding hame. I pin my coat with my dead mither's clasp and turn back towards the Border. The world is as it aye was, and our weird grips lichen to a gate.

I am sorry only I did not recover his father's ring. It will forever lie ayont the corbies' reach, round a white fingerbane in the depths of Liddiesdale.

In the howe the hassocks wet my ankles. I am entering the fringes of the mist, clutching the coin and brooch. In time there will be another song made, and in time it too will wear thin. Then there will be only an old road, a rickle of stones, the wind repeating on the borderline.

The haar clasps about me. I walk into it and am gane.

JAIRZINHO AND MY DAD

David McVey

'How come ye never tell us why ye don't live wi yer mum and dad?' said Eddie.

'Aye,' said wee John. 'Whit dae ye live wi yer auntie and uncle fur?'

'Jist because,' I said.

'His maw and da don't waant him!' said Freeky and everybody started laughing.

'They dae so!' I wouldn't cry even if they tried to make me.

'Where ur they, then?'

'Mind yer ain business.'

They forgot it soon enough. The World Cup had just finished and all we wanted to do was play football. We came to the field we called the Lannie. It was called that because of the steep slope down to the river at the back of the field: everybody tipped their rubbish down the slope. If the ball went over the edge and down the slope you had to sclim down after it through the rubbish and it felt like being in a landslide – or lannie, for short.

There were eight of us so we formed two teams of four.

'We'll play a two-fiver,' said Eddie, who always likes to organize things.

'I'll stay back,' said wee John, who was on my side. 'I'll go Jairzinho.'

'Jairzinho disnae play back. He goes forward and dribbles and beats everybody and scores.' Even though it was Donnie who said that he was right. Jairzinho was brilliant. Donnie was a diddy, though.

'He can play back if he waants tae cause he's Brazil's best player.'

'Naw he cannae. Carlos Alberto wid tell him tae go back up and score.' Daigie said that because Carlos Alberto was their captain. But Pele was their best player. He was the best player ever and Brazil was the best team ever. But Jairzinho was brilliant. I was Roberto Rivelino because I could hit the ball dead hard and straight.

We had only been playing for a few minutes when Jamie came through the lane and across the road to the field. He lived next door and he was really stupid.

'Andrew!' he shouted, 'Andrew Lawson! Yer Auntie Jean waants ye!'

It wasn't teatime yet. I couldn't think why my auntie wanted to see me. Had she found out about the broken door on the garden shed where I'd kicked the ball against it?

I followed Jamie back throught the lane with my tummy going all tight and squidgy like when my aunt made me take syrup of figs. I went in by the back door. Auntie Jean and Uncle Tommy were in the living-room. There was a strange man with them, wearing a suit and trying to smile. My mum was there as well. She lived not far away but she didn't come to see us often. I hated it when she did.

I hated her. And I hated my dad, too, though I hadn't seen him for years. It was all my dad's fault that they had split up. All my aunts and uncles and cousins said that and so I hated my dad. But I hated my mum too.

'This is Mr Crawford, Andrew,' said my auntie. 'He's your mum's lawyer. He's got something to tell you.'

Then she and Uncle Tommy went out of the room and I was left with this man and Mum.

'Hello, Andrew. Been playing football?' It was a stupid question to ask. I was covered in muck and wearing my Rangers strip. I didn't say anything.

'You know that I'm your mum's lawyer? Good. Well, your dad –' He stopped and looked at Mum for a minute. She just lit a fag. She smoked all the time. I hated the smell. 'Your dad has a lawyer as well. I've been talking to your dad's lawyer, with one of the judges in Edinburgh. You know what judges are? Very clever men who know what's right?'

I hated it when people talked to me like I was five or something. I'm eleven. And I'm not stupid.

'Well, we all decided that it would be good if your dad got a chance to take you somewhere for the day. What do you think? You don't have to go, but . . .'

'He'd bloody better no go,' said my mum.

'I'll swap ye Colin Bell and Francis Less fur yer packet o Munchies.' Eddie must have been hungry to give up two World Cup coins but I didn't want any more. I didn't know why people collected them, even though they came free with petrol. We all wanted England to lose. It was great when West Germany beat them in extra time. We didn't have a car but I still had about twelve of those stupid coins.

It was Wednesday night. We were at the summer gospel meeting that the church did. Not the old church with the old women and the boring minister. This was another, funny church. Lots of them were young and they smiled and had guitars. Some of the girls were lovely and wore short skirts and smelled of nice soap.

We sang songs and played games and there was a Bible talk. We all went because they gave out sweeties at the end. Even wee John went and he was a Catholic. Gary was one of the leaders from the church. He was young and told jokes and was good at football. He went up the front and got us to be quiet.

'OK, folks,' he said, 'let's all pray together now. You all know the Lord's Prayer?'

We bowed our heads except for Freeky, who always kept one eye open in case anyone knocked his sweeties. Then when it was hushed, we started.

'Our Father . . .'

'Right. Are ye listenin?' said my mum, 'We've tae be at the cross at half-nine. Ye've tae go up tae him yourself. I'll jist wait ootside Woolworths. He'll ask ye if ye waant tae go away fur the day, and you've tae say naw, right?'

I nodded.

'He'll probably ask ye again. You jist say naw again. Start greetin if ye can. If he tries tae grab ye it's a'right. Yer Uncle Alfie is gonnae be right by ye, kiddin on he's waitin fur a bus. Yer faither disnae know him.'

Uncle Alfie had boxed when he was in the army. He wasn't a real uncle, he was Mum's boyfriend.

'Whit if a bus comes? He'll look stupid if he disnae go for it.'

'Naw he'll no. He could be waitin fur the Mavis Valley bus.'

'Whit if it's the Mavis Valley bus that comes?'

'That's enough o yer bloody cheek.'

My mum lit a fag, put on her jacket, and went out of the house.

'Dae I have tae dae aa this?' I asked my Auntie Jean.

'Aye, son. It's the law.'

I went out and got my football and started kicking it against the shed. I tried to kid on it was my mum I was kicking, and then my dad. I hated them both. Why did they have to split up? Loads of mums and dads stayed together. Even if they weren't happy they did it. It was easy. You just stayed.

The ball bounced back to me. I gave it a Roberto Rivelino whack and kidded on I was aiming at my mum. And the next one was for my dad. It was all right for them. He was in the army now, and she worked as a packer in the woollens factory. It wasn't them that had to explain to the teacher why my sick note wasn't signed by my mum or my dad, or who had to listen to everybody shouting, 'Yer mammy disnae waant ye! Yer mammy disnae waant ye!' When I'm big I'm going to get married and I'm going to stay that way. If I'm lucky I'll marry Jennifer Scullion. She's gorgeous. I'll show them how easy it is to stay together.

My aunt gave me toast. I couldn't eat it. I felt as if I wanted to go to the toilet. I hadn't slept all night.

We got the local bus over to the Cross. Uncle Alfie was already there. He had Brylcreem in his hair. You could see it gleaming even from where we were, just outside Woolworths. We stood there waiting. My mum lit a fag, smoked it, and then lit another; three buses went past towards Glasgow: a Twechar, a Waterside, and a Dunfermline. You could tell the Dunfermline bus easy because it was red instead of blue. Uncle Alfie was still waiting there.

Then my dad appeared, from round the corner. He had a car and must have parked there. I didn't recognize him. But my mum knew him. 'On ye go!' she said and gave me a wee push in the back.

I walked towards him. He just stood there. I was shaking. I thought I might pee myself. 'Never go up and speak to strangers,' they said usually. But my dad was a stranger.

I stopped just in front of him. He was tall and fair-haired. I looked more like Mum.

'Hello, Andrew.' I didn't even recognize his voice. 'Remember me?' I nodded. 'Are you coming away for the day? I've got the car – a Cortina. We can go to the seaside.'

'No. I don't want to.'

'Aye ye do. Yer mum told ye not to.' He spoke funny, sort of half-English, like Denis Law.

'I don't. I don't waant to go.'

'Aye ye do. C'mon. C'mere.' He took a step towards me. I turned my head a bit to see Uncle Alfie lean off the railings and move a bit closer as another bus went past. My dad saw my head move and looked over his shoulder at Uncle Alfie.

'C'mon. Ye'll enjoy it.'

'Naw.'

'Come on.'

I tried to start crying. It was easy. I wasn't frightened or anything but crying was easy. It was Saturday and the town was busy and people kept going past. They looked at me crying and then at Dad.

'All right. Have it your own way. I'll see ye again, son.

OK?' He looked up and over my head at my mum, who'd come a bit closer. I was frightened that some of my pals would see me before my dad went. But he turned quickly, brushed past Uncle Alfie – he gave him a real look – and disappeared round the corner.

I went back home in the bus with Mum and Uncle Alfie. They didn't speak to me, and they didn't come back into the house. Mum just unlocked the door for me and away they went.

I felt like crying again. Aunt Jean and Uncle Tommy were away for the messages. I was on my own. Instead I picked up my football comic. There was a picture of Carlos Alberto scoring the fourth Brazil goal against Italy. It was brilliant.

BEAUTIFUL FOX

Ruth Thomas

Moonlight shines through the curtains but it doesn't wake the old man. He is awake already, having a conversation in his head. 'Hot this evening dear,' he is saying to his wife. 'Hot. I can't sleep.'

'Well, it's July,' says his wife. 'You should take that blanket off the bed.'

'Yes,' he says, 'I should do that,' but he just lies there, in the square of moonlight, with his eyes open.

After a while he gets out of bed, pulls the drawstring tighter on his pyjamas and walks into the hall. It is so curious at this time of night. There are bookshelves on either side of him and they are like cliffs, blue and cold. The plants on the shelves hang their leaves out like the paws of nocturnal animals. His feet are bare and the floorboards are cold and waxy, but he can feel them better like that; he can avoid the ones that creak. He walks in a zig-zag to the kitchen, and his wife is still talking. 'Why don't you make yourself a cup of tea?' she is saying. 'It'll make you feel better.' He switches the kitchen light on and takes the kettle to the sink. On the wall there is a picture of a saucepan and some onions, re-appearing every ten tiles or so, like a recurring nightmare. He stares at the picture while the water runs.

There is a sound outside, a dog barking, or maybe it is even a fox; foxes come into the city these days but usually in cold weather, in the winter. They come and look for food. He and Jessica saw that fox once, one night in December, just gliding above the snow, and it was beautiful; they had just stood, arm-in-arm, holding their breath, watching. Orange against white. That evening the snow had started falling, and the city had been covered up. He remembers the way the fox looked at them, the way it turned its sharp face.

The old man opens the cupboard and looks at tea boxes. There are so many of them. 'What shall I have?' he says. 'Shall I have Lemon Zinger? Do I want to be zinged at three-forty-five in the morning? Or rosehip and apple? Or spearmint?' His daughter made some pasta thing with garlic last night, and garlic disagrees with him. It makes him feel bad in the middle of the night. He thinks the spearmint would be best for his stomach, but ordinary tea, that is better for his mind, for his heart. He lifts a mug off the mug tree and when the kettle has boiled he puts a tea-bag in the mug and stirs it around. He likes his tea nice and dark, not the kind his daughter makes; that is just white liquid. 'This is the land of milk and water,' says his wife, but no, it's not his wife, it's him saying that; his wife liked weak tea.

Everything sounds loud at this time in the morning, even sipping. Even the quietness is loud. The fridge clicks in its sleep, in one of its strange, freezing dreams, and it makes him jump. Tea falls on the lino. 'Hell,' he says, but there is no reply. His wife is not there any more; she has gone off again, suddenly, without telling him, she has just slipped away. 'Come back,' he says, but there is silence. Every time she disappears he is afraid she will not return. Cold air blows through his pyjama shirt, but the window is shut. The glass is black, black, reflecting nothing.

The old man walks with his tea into the sitting room. Living room, his son-in-law calls it, but his son-in-law does not live in it. 'Right,' the old man says to the hi-fi in the corner, to the rows of CDs, to the picture of boats in a harbour. 'What do I do now?' he says. He can hear a seagull screaming above the roof. Night-time always has seagulls in it now but every time the scream-ing sounds new. He looks through the window and he can't see it for a while, the seagull, but then he does; it is standing, huge and truculent on the roof of the car mechanic's. *Tired Of Your Tyres? Exhausted By Your Exhaust? Let Us Refresh You.* Does it say that in the adverts? Yes, he thinks it says that. 'Ah,' says the seagull, and it raises its grey wings and flies away. The sky is layered with clouds but it is going to be hot tomorrow, he can feel it.

When he turns round, he sees a woman standing in the doorway. She is wearing a red dressing gown, hold-ing it around her as if she is cold.

'Dad?' says the woman.

'I just made myself a cup of tea,' says the old man.

'Are you all right, Dad?' says the woman. 'I heard you talking to someone,' she says.

She walks towards him. She has kind eyes; brown, brown, like chocolate. He loves his daughter, but some-times he can't remember what her name is.

'You're crying,' she says.

'No.' he says, 'no, I'm not. Do you remember when we . . . ?'

'What?' she says.

'The fox,' he says. 'Do you remember when we saw the fox? That winter?'

'You should be in bed,' she says. 'You're tired.'

'No,' he says. 'It was beautiful.'

'I remember you and Mum telling me about it,' says the woman. 'I remember you sitting at the edge of the bed and telling me about it.'

'Yes,' he says, 'it was a beautiful fox.'

'Let's get you back to bed,' says his daughter, and she puts her hand on his arm.

There are things he wants to know. Why he is here, he wants to know that. Also where he is. He has worked out that he must be near the sea. This is a start. 'I'm just going outside for a minute,' he says. 'I just would like to be outside.'

'But you're only wearing pyjamas,' says the woman.

'So?' he says and he wonders how long ago it was that she grew up. He walks quickly into the hallway. The hallway smells of air freshener and garlic, a foreign smell. It makes him feel unwell. He turns the latch and opens the front door wide. He breathes. There is already light in the sky, a quiet, pink light, and the seagulls are flying in swathes now, back to the coast. It looks as if they are pulling some big dark curtain with them as they go. The garden is losing whatever it has in the middle of the night; its sadness, and a square of yellow has appeared suddenly on the pathway. This means that the man, the son-in-law is up; he is up and switching the light on and he will be downstairs any minute. He will be downstairs wearing aftershave. 'Quick,' says the old man.

'What are you doing?' says the woman. She is standing behind him and holding on to his elbow, damn it, as if he is about to keel over. The old man does not reply. He peers into the green bushes at the end of the garden. Upstairs there is the sound of water running, and a radio. The radio is singing:

> What shall we do with the drunken sailor,
> What shall we do with the drunken sailor,
> What shall we do with the drunken sailor,
> Ear-ly in the morning?

'Yes,' says the old man, 'there it is.'

He sees it suddenly; it is walking like treacle through the bushes. Soundless. A small, orange fox. 'See?' he says. 'See where I'm pointing?'

'Where?' says the woman. It is no use trying to stop him now. She remembers the way he used to point things out when she was small; how she would look the length of his blue-jumpered arm and into the sky, trying to see what he had seen. She had forgotten that: how much time she had spent with him, trying to locate things in the distance. 'Oh yes,' she would say, 'I can see it,' whatever it was, a butterfly or a bird of prey. And often she would pretend, just so she didn't look stupid.

'Can you see it now?' her father says, and he is still looking at something in the leaves. 'Where?' she says. She follows the stretch of his arm but her eyesight is not good in the dark and she can hardly even make out the gate, or the houses opposite. She will have to lie again, to make him happy; she will have to pretend that she has seen some animal moving quickly; some creature with glowing eyes. 'Look. There,' says her father, and she smiles. There is nothing. She stares hard into the flower-beds.

'Dad,' she says, and she sighs because she is trying to think of something else to say, something that won't annoy him or confuse him or make him sad, and it is so difficult seeing him like this, the way he is now; she is sighing because of that, when she hears her mother talking. Suddenly, for the first time in months, she can hear her mother, speaking in her slow way. 'Dear man,' she is saying, 'dear man,' and the words are so clear. She has missed her mother's voice more than anything.

'Can you see it?' her father is saying. 'Beautiful fox', and his face has one tear, running diagonally. There is the noise upstairs of the woman's husband shutting a door and beginning to walk downstairs, and before he gets to the hall and asks what they are doing, standing there letting all the air in, she says, 'Yes, yes I can,' because there is a fox, definitely, she can see it now, running away from them, away from the houses, something bright and good.

FLESH AND BLOOD

Anne Donovan

And they aw lived happy ever efter.

Nae matter the story, nae matter whit terrible things huv happened, that's aye how it ends. The princess gets her man, the goodie beats the baddie, the nurse merries the doactor. An Ah wis a sucker fur stories, couldnae get enough a them, heid never oot a book unless Ah wis at the pictures, lost in that celluloid world where aw the colours are brighter than the real thing.

Angela!
   Am cummin.
   Get yer heid oot that book an get the ironin done. Am gaun tae ma work.
   In a minute.
   No in a minute. This minute.

They made a big deal ooty that, me an ma stories, a bitty a fantasist they said at the trial, didnae really know whit she wis daein. Under a loaty pressure at the time efter whit hud happened, didnae know the difference between right an wrang. Yon lawyer wus a smert wumman, pulled oot aw the stoaps fur me; hormones, grief trauma, deprived background (ma ma wis mad

157

at that but the lawyer tellt her it wis jist fur the jury), the loat.

My client's father left home when she was six and she and her two brothers were brought up by her mother, who worked at nights as a cleaner.

An who am Ah tae say that she wisnae right, fur the problem wi livin yer life is that ye see it fae inside yer ain heid an when y're in the middle a sumpn, whether it's a sair heid or a bad mood, ye canny look at it objectively. It's dead easy if it's sumdy else; we're aye saying *whit's he gettin aw wurked up aboot?* or *she's better aff wioot him,* but it disnae wurk oan yersel the same way. Ye canny feel sumdy else's pain or joy the way they dae, even when ye love them. Ah used taw think ye could, that wis whit love wis, the end tae the loneliness a bein alive. Ah mind bein in love an lookin intae his eyes, that blue they were, his eyes, an thinking he must feel the same as me, how could he no, that wis whit wis in aw the stories.

Of course Ah love ye, Angela. C'moan, d'you no love me?
    Course Ah dae. Aw, Ah don't know, ur ye sure it's aw right?
    Ah'll be careful, hoanest. We're gettin engaged as soon as we've saved up. C'moan.
    Oh, Peter.

But the next bit wisnae in the story fur Ah fell pregnant an he dumped me.

Every story hus its bad bits though; the heroine hus a rival fur her man's love or the prince hus tae dae some tests tae prove he's worthy of the princess, an Ah assumed this wis jist a setback in ma story, an obstacle in ma path. Ah pined fur ma man fur a while but then Hazel wis born, an it wis as if Ah'd lived aw ma life in a country where the only flooers were buttercups an Ah'd aye thoat how beautiful an perfect they were, till wan day sumdy gied me a big bunch a roses.

Ah never knew, Ah don't think emdy can know till it happens tae them, jist whit it means tae huv a wean that wee an helpless, depending oan ye fur everything. And you made her, oot a nothin it seems, nothin but a few words, two boadies daein sumpn oot a love or fur their ain pleasure or whitever. An fae that few minutes came this perfect wee bein, bundled up in a shawl so's aw ye could see wis her eyes, hazel eyes, lik mines. Shinin lik stars, they were, as if they'd absorbed everythin in the wurld an reflected it back at ye. An when she wis sleepin the eyelashes curled oan her cheeks lik feathers an her breath wis a cloud driftin ower the sky oan a still day; ye kept lookin an lookin an ye could hardly see the movement.

When Hazel wis new born Ah kept wakin her tae check she wis still alive, Ah couldnae believe she wis that quiet an still. Ah'd gie her a wee kiss oan the cheek, an her eyes wid open, lookin aw roon lik wanny they princesses that gets woken up efter a hunner years. Ma mammy said Ah wis daft an the wean wid get girny if her sleep wis disturbed, but Ah couldnae help masel. Still, it's lik everythin else, ye get used tae it, ye'd probly get used tae heaven after a few weeks an start wishin ye could go doon Argyle Street oan a Saturday. So ye stoap wakin her up an ye take it fur grantit she's that quiet an motionless in her cot, a good baby, a lovely baby, sleepin said sound an contentit. Then wan morning she disnae wake up.

My client's child died on February 15th. She was well fed, well looked after and no specific cause of death was identified. In other words she was the victim of Sudden Infant Death Syndrome, what the layperson would call a cot death.

A cot death. A syndrome. A statistic.

An in the absence ae a fairy godmother tae wave her magic wand an make it better, they sent me tae grief counsellin, three sessions Ah hud in a wee room hidden away at the endy a coarridor wi a squeaky linoleum flair. The wumman looked lik the heidmistress at ma primary school but she tried tae be nice.

How do you feel?
  Och, you know.
  You must be feeling depressed.

Ah feel as if ma insides huv been taorn oota me, actually, as if sumdy hud ripped ma guts oot wi a rid-hot perra pliars, an left me raw an bleedin an burnin.

It's quite natural, you know.
  Uh huh.
  You mustn't blame yourself, there was nothing you could do. The social worker said you were a very good mother.

They said that at the trial tae, how good Ah wis wi ma ain wean, an Ah'd nae intention a hurtin the wee wan, Ah wis confused, Ah thoat she wis mines. That's in the

stories tae, the weans get swapped at birth an the princess gets broat up as the kitchen maid, but even Ah
wisnae taken in by that wan, fur whit mother disnae
know her ain flesh an blood. Ah knew she wisnae Hazel,
Ah knew when Ah took her oot the pram; she hud blue
eyes an her skin felt different an she smellt different.
Even a sheep knows the smell a her ain lamb an if it
dies an the shepherd wants her tae suckle a motherless
wan, he pits the new lamb in the deid lamb's fleesh.

*In a state of extreme distress and confusion at the loss of her own
child, my client lifted Baby Cowan out of a pram which had been
left outside Boots in the Argyle Street Shopping Centre on the
afternoon of May 25th, the date of her own child's birth.*

Ah took her hame an wrapped her in Hazel's shawl an
held her close tae me an smellt ma wean's smell an felt
the rise an fall ae a baby's breath an the warmth ae a
baby's kin, but never did Ah imagine fur wan minute
she wis ma wean, it jist made me feel better fur a while.
That's all, it jist made me feel better.

Ah couldnae say that at the trial; Ah hud tae listen
tae them talkin aboot me as if Ah wis a character in ma
ain life. An it made nae sense, jist as the stories make
nae sense tae me noo, fur there hus tae be a point tae
stories, a reason how wan thing happens an no anither.
But there's nae reason fur whit happened tae Hazel.
An in a story the character hus tae huv a motivation an
it's no enough tae say that ye stole a wean oot a pram
jist because haudin her made ye feel better.

Even if it's true.

PECAN MACINTYRE

Tom Bryan

'Bigger than a coffin, not as wide as a church door.' Who said that? Marcuse? He must have been talking about my box room – my home, my world for most of my life so far. I am now closing three doors to that life.

Door One. Box-room door, opens to the kitchen.

Door Two. Kitchen door, opens to the hall.

Door Three. Opens from the hall to the landing. Our 'front' door.

Flat 3 (TCF). Top floor, centre flat, or, third floor, centre flat.

Key locks the door of hard dark varnish, peeling like black sunburnt skin around the tarnished brass name-plate – our name: MACINTYRE. I leave it for the new owners. Who knows. Maybe they will be 'MacIntyre' as well. I drop the key through the letter box.

One last look. The landing. TLF. The family 'LIS-TER', here before me, still here, but no nameplate on TRF – a succession of students, flatmates and lodgers.

Then, down the stairs: door bells, iron rails, peeling green pastel walls against the dark stone of scrubbed stairs and floor, scrubbed to a white grain, like a salt-sand beach, and down to the bright green blistered door, which opens to the street, never locked in all my days there, long final dark hall leading to it also scrubbed – the smell of Dettox only slightly stronger than the smell of drunkard piss, dog fur and exhaust fumes coming in from the street.

I am on the street, suitcase in hand; like so many of my people before me; taxi, Waverley Station, bus, airport.

Cabbie. Ginger like me. A bit older. I'm thirty-two.

America, eh?

I have a job there.

Lucky bugger. Nae life here.

(I don't tell him I may not stay there.) I work in Disease Control – plenty of diseases to keep me busy – but I may not stay. Not for me: Disney World, the Grand Canyon, Florida. I will go to the deep red clay of Georgia, find a pecan tree and stroke its rough brown bark and down leaves; then I will either remember, forget or understand – and any of those things will be good.

Thomas J. MacIntyre, my old man, now dead from the fags; he got greyer and smaller every year and coughed and died. Wee squat dark man – he always said he was the last of the Picts – a good man, hard worker, the eternal punter. Forklift driver and mechanic. From Inverness, a long time ago (for his sins, a Caley supporter) and I can still hear his Inverness speech – 'the purest English spoken' he would laugh – and I remember when computers were becoming popular hearing him first say the word 'computer'. Pure English? 'Campewerr'. Maybe. I miss him.

Mother, Rona, bonny and red, grew up in the same flat in the same room as me, died two months ago to the day. She was the flat, the cladding, the mortar and dark wood of the place, and I could never believe it would survive her, that I would one day drop the key through a letter box for another owner; the final soft thud of it, from myself, Kevin 'Box Room' MacIntyre.

My father was from a big family. His brother James, my uncle – merchant navy, wanderer, supposed flawed genius, married a woman in Savannah, Georgia, then unsuccessfully farmed peaches and peanuts before settling on pecan nuts, becoming, we'd heard, 'The Pecan King of Georgia'.

And one spring day, James MacIntyre, ex-merchant seaman and Pecan King, crossed our polished brass threshold, bringing a rust-red cloth bag of shelled pecan nuts for us. His daughter Catherine was with him. She was five years older than me. I was six.

James was tall, thin and dark – entirely unlike my father. After greetings and enquiries the adults went through the door on the right into the living room and Catherine and myself went left into the kitchen and sat down at the table, facing each other from the table ends.

Catherine, thin and dark in a light blue dress, curly black hair and eyes like a cow's – liquid and the perfect brown for her brown skin. A face as open as a deep pool, though at age six, I only remember staring at her.

'I'm Catherine. But nobody calls me that. Everybody calls me Pecan – they say I'm like a pecan pie: hard, dark but sweet. You're my first cousin, Kevin.'

Aye.

My dad says that all the time.

Eh?

Says that all the time too.

Pecan?

164

Not Puh-can, but *Pee*-can.

She would see a short (too white) freckled boy, hair the colour of old copper water pipes; a little scabby boy of no interest to her, my legs not even reaching from the seat to the floor. Our kitchen would interest her more. The tallest and largest room in the flat, all white, natural tiles of beige; heavy drop-leaf table ('early Depression' my mother called it) in one small corner nearest my box-room bedroom; a long wall with sink and cabinets. Opposite was the cream-coloured Raeburn, above it the pulley to dry the clothes. At the far wall was a window going from the floor to the tall ceiling, where every visitor would stand at some time, viewing the dark slates and chimney pots of Edinburgh to the far horizon, ending in the bulk of Arthur's Seat.

And Pecan was there. Her curly head haloed by the purple light of Edinburgh in the spring, a still brown life against the glistening roofs; against the hard slow smoke of the city, making the old volcano seem alive with the illusion of smoke coming from it and not from the city below.

'Y'all got a real mountain in yo kitchen window – a real live mountain.'

Her back to me, the curves of her in the soft dress, visible in the window light, in the centre of the slow, drifting smoke . . .

We heard the adults laughing in the other room and on that day, Pecan MacIntyre took my sweating freckled hand in her long exquisite fingers out into the spring evening of Edinburgh. Turn right, cross one street, past the fruit and vegetable stalls, to the newsagent for sweets. She let go of my hand then, leaving a pale ring around my knuckles.

She took my hand again on the street. I heard a window open across the street, at Iain Doig's house.

'Look at Kevin MacIntyre, holding hands with a nigger.'

I felt Pecan's long fingers tighten, tense against my sweating skin. She let go of my hand only when we got back to the flat. I sat crunching sweets while Pecan took her place at the window again.

'Pecan, what's a nigger?'

Her dark eyes burned through my freckles. I never asked her that question again.

I learned later Uncle James had married a black woman from Macon, Georgia. Pecan looked just like her mother.

We fed the pecan nuts to the hesitant squirrels in the Royal Botanic Gardens and put the rest out for the hungry birds of winter, but the red bag of nuts never seemed to diminish much. I did some growing in the meantime, freckles now confused by acne, my room shrinking like a goldfish bowl as I grew. My box-room opened to the kitchen in the wall opposite its large window so that my door, fully open, gave me that window view; no other views were possible from my box room: one bed along one wall of the rectangle; chest of drawers against the short wall; small wardrobe and shelves along the wall separating my room from the kitchen. Beyond my chest of drawers must have been the bedroom of the adjoining flat for I could often hear Mr and Mrs Lister on their bed, springs creaking. I heard the rising and falling of grunting and sighing, reminding me of a kitchen kettle shaking as it reaches boiling point, then fading to a satisfied hiss.

*   *   *

Uncle James came a few more times, on his own. He was exporting pecan nuts to Britain now. He always left us a grainy red cloth bag of pecans, which vanished slowly into the tight paws of the grey squirrels of the Botanic Garden.

I was thirteen and Pecan was eighteen when they next came.

Pecan's mother came with them that time. Aunt Sally. Long tall Sally. She had on a light blue summer dress. Her hair was plaited down her back. She was black and striking. At thirteen, I was taller than both my parents. Pecan was now only slightly taller than me. She was dressed in a red flared skirt and white blouse.

(Some things never change in Scotland. Children to the kitchen, adults to the living room.) Pecan stood tall against the window.

'Well, Kevin, do you remember the last time you saw me?'

'I do. We went out for sweets.'

She laughed and walked over to her flight bag by the table.

'My dad says you're into football and music. Don't know much about football but thought you might like some Georgia music.'

It was a treasure she emptied on to the hard scratched wood of the kitchen table. Albums of Little Richard and James Brown.

I mumbled a thanks, still in awe of my dark cousin, who was back at the window.

'Kevin, see all the chimneys, all that smoke. People laughing, crying, loving out there. Standing here, we only see the smoke. Lingers, then blows away. Like us.

Through all that you got a mountain in the distance. Some folks have to look hard through all that smoke and rain to see that mountain there . . .'

Then her voice lowered.

'All those dreams out there, over the roof.'

Pecan, tall and lean against the window, the rainbow prism of a small tear on her left brown cheekbone.

The door opened, the moment gone. It was Aunt Sally.

'Kevin, I'm gonna show yo momma what to do with pecans. Imagine feedin' pecans to squirrels . . . That's good human food we talking' about – soul food.'

My mother hovered giggling, small and red against the window. Pecan and I sat at the kitchen table while our mothers worked on the counter top, mixing and laughing in the dark shadow of Arthur's Seat with: butter, brown sugar, three eggs (well-beaten) corn syrup? No? Treacle will do, salt, chopped pecan nuts, vanilla. Bake very hot, cool down, serve with cream.

The taste was warm, soft, sugary, yet hard and dark, crunchy, perfect with hot tea; all adults eating quietly, happily at the kitchen table against the dark angry purple of the old volcano.

And an awkward goodbye kiss from me on Pecan, my nose glancing off her cheek where lingered a smell something like sugar and pecan, a cheek the colour of milky tea, me still beaming bright red long after the door was closed.

Pecan came one last time.

I was seventeen, preparing for exams, preparing for university that autumn. It was April and my parents had gone to Inverness for the weekend. I was at the kitchen table. Door bell, Pecan at the door. As tall as last time, in faded flared jeans, short-sleeved light blue blouse, hair in magnificent Afro, bordered by a bright red and black patterned headband. We hugged, went into the kitchen for tea.

Pecan said she had been in London, preparing to go to Biafra as part of a food and medical relief team, hoping to get through the invading Nigerian troops. She'd come up to Edinburgh on her free weekend.

'Kevin, the Biafrans are a nation of poets and musicians – dreamers and thinkers – and the Nigerian government wants to starve the entire nation to death, with British and American help, of course. I'm going with a relief team to try to get supplies through. It's unofficial and dangerous – in the middle of a war.'

I told her of my plans to be a doctor.

'Good man, cousin. I like it. A doctor who can jive to James Brown!'

She placed the very first Allman Brothers record on the table – still impossible to get in Edinburgh.

She stood at the window. Edinburgh spring afternoon – sun, rain and sky all burled together – and we drank wine, made a pecan pie, studied for my exam and played James Brown records: 'Ain't no drag – Kevin's got a brand-new bag . . . Hey, Momma, hey, hey . . .'

The wine went to my head – I wasn't used to it – and I remember waking, fully clothed, in my box-room bed. Pecan must have put me there, then gone off to sleep in the living room or other bedroom.

About dawn, I woke, needing the loo. My door was slightly ajar. I could see the early light coming through the kitchen window. Pecan was there. She was dressed in a long white nightgown, her arms to the window, her back to me. I could see her strong dark body through the light cotton. She looked like an angel or a moth, flattened against the glass, crucified. I could hear her crying softly.

I know I was not meant to see or hear her. I did nothing though I wanted to comfort her in some way. I pretended I did not see and quietly turned away from the half-open door. I fell asleep. She was gone when I awoke.

I never saw Pecan MacIntyre again. She was last seen alive by the British Red Cross on a dusty famine road. She was on foot, heading for the interior of a country whose people were becoming the smoke of a twilight dream, dispersed for ever in the flame of war.

Smoke, blown across the rooftops of the world.

BLASTED BY SANDS

Mary McCabe

The shakes. The stink. The flies.

Outside was snow on the street; one of the horses skited on the way and nearly took a tumble. Inside there's a fire, but the room's that big there's lacings of frost on all the windows.

Forty beds reeking and heaving; devils dancing about and between. Devils waiting for souls; now and again they catch one. Young lad two beds along just left feet first, greeting woman trailing behind.

Sometimes they're fly – they come in with a wee bowl of soup or a cup of water. My gob is paper, my thrapple Fordyce's furnace, but I know better than to take their hellish concoctions.

Once one tried it on with me; sucked me into the middle of the bed like a whirlpool, then up in the air like a peerie. Round and round till I was dizzy, birling me by my nightshirt tail, corner to corner, up and down, side to side. I grat my teeth and saw it through to laugh in its face when it had to let me fall.

Just as well. Willie could leave the school and Fordyce would give him a start, but a boy's pay would never go round four. It would be the poorshouse for the rest.

Worst is the long night, nothing to see but the shadows on the wall, nothing to hear but girning, nothing to smell but sweat, piss and boke, nothing to think on but the weans and whether I've lost my place at the foundry.

Still, behind the night is aye the dawn. One day I feel better and rise, and scouk out when the nurse's back's turned.

Somehow I win home. The devils are after me yet; barring the closemouth against me; still I'm drawn by hearth and family, up the stair and into the kitchen. But here! What's the game? Without asking, they've done away with the range. How will we warm ourselves now?

Just when I'm pondering on this Agnes walks in. We smile at each other and I say, 'I'm hame, hen.' I open my arms to her, but she crosses to the jawbox at the window. She turns on the tap and washes her hands.

Is it really Agnes? It's her height and colouring, but something's off the reel. Can it be another blasted devil? Do they never call it a day?

I reach out, feart in case it turns and grins on me with its damned mouth.

Agnes lets out a scraich. She chitters and all the hairs on her arm stand up. Then she's away out the door, bubbling and bawling.

I stand by my hearth, trying to make sense of this. Syne a young wife comes in; behind hops not-quite-Agnes. She points to the sink. 'I was over there when I felt it.'

'There's nothing there, Debbie.' The woman waves vaguely in my direction.

She carries plates into the red-recess and I notice the bed's away. In its place is a table with three chairs. I shout, 'Whit's daen wi the lassies' bed? Whaur are Agnes and Jessie to pit their heids?'

They pay me no more heed than if I was the wind up the lum. When they've finished setting the table they dauner out arm-in-arm.

Fiends or folk, they strut about my hame and make me a bit of dirt in my own kitchen. I'll gar them tak tent! I smash a plate on the floor. The noise brings them peching ben.

'Was it an earthquake?' asks Agnes, or Debbie, or whatever.

'I maybe didn't put it right on the table,' says the wife.

'I'm scared,' says the lassie.

'Nothing to be scared of,' says the wife, and chitters.

By night, I go ben the house. The lobby's changed, with another room added, though how they've fitted it in atween us and Mrs McGregor's I don't know. In the front room recess sleeps a stranger. A beardy, hair red as carrots spread over my bolster, wife asleep at his back. Christ knows what they've been at, fornicating in my marriage-bed. Demons the lot of them.

I grab him by the thrapple to heist him out.

'Uggglugglug . . . !' He reaches and the place floods with light.

"What's up, Brian?" asks the wife.

I dance about, bawling 'Get out of my bed, you cursed crew!'

'Don't know,' he mumbles. 'Something choking me.'

'Just a dream,' soothes the wife. And do they no douse the light, turn their backs on me and start up their snoring again!

Night after night they stare at a wee box full of moving pictures. I find out how to make the pictures go away and come back, and I take to pushing the button in again and again. That gars them grue – they run about scraiching like rats, blaming each other, while I laugh till I'm like to burst. But where's the weans? I've speired at them and bawled at them till I'm black in the face.

One day they bring in another geezer, baldy and shilpit as a brush. He spots me right away. 'What do you want?' he asks, as if I'm the intruder.

'Get you all to Hell out of it,' I bawl. 'Devils the lot of you!'

'Who's there?' asks Brian. 'What can you see?'

'These people aren't devils,' says Baldy to me. 'They've bought this house. They want to live here in peace. Who are you?'

'I'm Johnny MacPherson!' I shout. 'This is ma hame and ma weans are Christ knows whaur. I pay ma rent and no bugger dare sell this roof frae ower ma heid!'

Then they're gone. Back to the kingdom of hell. My hame's my own and not my own, crammed with other folks' gear. White things in the kitchen, all spotless, though I've yet to see yon dame scrubbin like poor Ina used to.

Outside is altered too. The middle door in the landing, Mrs McGregor's single end, is away. Instead, my house has another door, leading to a bath and WC. What they've done with Mrs McGregor I can only jalouse. But they'll not get me. I'm too quick, on the roof in one blink, the back court the next. All grassed over, the midden tidy in a wee biggen. Where's the ash and the mire and the weans dreeping down the dyke? *Where's the weans?*

Night follows day six times but no living soul disturbs my peace. Then Baldy returns and with him an old wife, ninety if she's a day.

'Johnny,' says Baldy, 'your daughter Agnes has a message for you.'

'No!' I shout. 'Never. You'll no make a clown oota Johnny MacPherson!'

'Paw?' quavers the old dame. 'Paw? D'ye hear me?'

'He hears you,' says Baldy.

'Paw? You're deid, Paw. You passed away long ago.' She turns to Baldy. 'Ah feel that daft yatterin to an empty kitchen.'

'You're okay,' says Baldy. 'Talk about the family.'

'Efter ye died, Paw, Willie stertit at the foundry and Auntie Beattie took me to help in her hoose. Where is he?'

'He's standing over by the freezer.''

'Whit way can you see him and Ah canny?'

'Ah canny credit ony o this!'' I thunder. 'Bloody liars the lotta yese!'

'I don't think he knows he's dead,' says Baldy.

'Ye died in the fever ward,' says the old dame. 'Mind the fever ward?'

'Where's ma weans?'' I shout. It's like bawling through glass. I scud a picture off the wall and they both jump sky-high.

'Is that the whole family?' asks Baldy.

'Davie and Jess went to the Quarrier's Homes. They posted them to Canada for a fresh start. The boys are passed away now, Paw. I lost my ain man, but Ah've three weans and five grand-weans and Ah'm

175

great-granny to two. Willie's lassies drop by sometimes. And Ah keep in touch wi Jessie in Winnipeg – she was back ower four times but noo she's no fit.'

Could it be? Right enough, things are no natural at all. it's all wrong the way I get to where I want by wishing it. Everything in the house new and altered – then this creature with the clapped-in jaws making out she's Agnes that I last saw with a white pinny and a ribbon in her hair. There must be a wheen of years lost in by. What did they do with the years?

'The image is fading,' says Baldy. He opens the kitchen door and in troop Brian and his wife. 'I've tried to make the spirit understand that it's dead,' he tells them. 'With luck you'll have no more bother.'

'We'd better not,' says the wife, 'or this house goes into the property pages next week.'

Where to, now? By wanting I could get, but I don't know what to want. Do I follow the old dame home? Agnes she might be, but she's no my Agnes, no my wee Agnes. She's that decrepit, if I give her the fleg when she's on her own she could drop deid hersel. I wouldny want to be the death of my own daughter. To Winnipeg, to seek out Jessie? Same story.

The demons have made themselves scarce at last. They know when they're on a loser. Johnny Mac-Pherson was too much man for them. I'm free.

Fresh strength. I turn my face upwards and make for the clouds. If the tales are true I'll maybe meet up with poor Ina. Failing that, there's the moon and the stars. Johnny MacPherson, never in life past Yoker, past Airdrie, will travel yet!

BIOGRAPHICAL NOTES

TOM BRYAN was born in Canada in 1950 but now lives in Strathkanaird, Wester Ross. A long-time resident in Scotland, he is a widely published poet and fiction writer and a former writing fellow for Aberdeenshire. This is his first story to appear in *Scottish Short Stories*.

JOHN CUNNINGHAM was born in Edinburgh in 1934. A retired farmer, his novel *Leeds to Christmas* was published by Polygon in 1990.

ANNE DONOVAN was born in 1955 and brought up in Coatbridge, Lanarkshire. She studied at Glasgow University and lives in Glasgow where she works as a teacher. Writing mainly prose fiction in Scots and English, her stories have appeared in *New Writing Scotland 14* and the 1997 volume of *The Flamingo Book of New Scottish Writing*.

BILL DUNCAN was born in Fife in 1953 and lives in Dundee. He has had non-fiction, poetry and prose published in a range of journals and magazines. 'Yin Yang' is his first published short story, and the first story he has written.

JONATHAN FALLA writes and nurses in Edinburgh, having lived in many tropical countries including

Sudan. His previous work includes stage plays, films for the BBC, and a study of ethnic rebels in Burma.

MOIRA FORSYTH lives in Dingwall, has just joined the editorial team of *Northwards* magazine, and chairs the Dingwall Writers' Group. A published poet, her stories have appeared in *Northwards* and the New Writing Scotland anthology, 1995, *Last Things First.*

LIZBETH GOWANS was born in Edinburgh. A childhood among the Scottish hills, where her father had herdings, provides material for much of her writing. She now lives in Yorkshire, where she is a part-time literature tutor for the WEA. Her work has been included in previous volumes of *Scottish Short Stories* and *New Writing Scotland* and she has had articles published in the *Scots Magazine.*

ANDREW GREIG is a full-time writer living mostly in Orkney and the Lothians. A published poet and novelist, he has also written books on mountaineering.

LAURA J. HIRD was born and lives in Edinburgh. Her work has been published in anthologies (*Children of Albion Rovers*, Canongate; *Typical Girls*, Hodder and Stoughton) and numerous magazines both in Britain and abroad. Her first collection, *Nail and Other Stories*, was published by Canongate in October 1997.

ANTHONY LAMBERT was born in 1944 in Tasmania, but has spent the last 25 years living on the Isle of Skye. An ex-teacher, seaman, builder, manager, fisherman, his stories and poems have appeared in *Spectrum, Orbis,*

Northwords and several newspapers. His first novel, *Stylus*, is currently under preparation for publication.

DAVID MCALPINE CUNNINGHAM was born in Ayrshire in 1970. He is currently working at Glasgow University, from which he has a Ph.D. in English Literature and is close to completing his first children's book.

MARY MCCABE was born in Glasgow in 1950, where she still lives and works as a Careers Adviser. She has also written a novel, *Everwinding Times*, three radio plays, a children's book and various short stories and articles.

LORN MACINTYRE was born in Argyll and is a full-time writer. He has had many short stories and several novels published.

DAVID MCVEY's home town is Kirkintilloch. Currently working in the Distance Learning Unit of the University of Paisley, he now lives in Milton of Campsie. He has had many stories and articles published in England, Scotland and Ireland.

G. A. PICKIN has a degree in archaeology and is married with twin daughters. She has lived in America, Mexico, Kenya, Libya, England and Wales, but currently resides in south west Scotland.

TOM RAE was born in Glasgow in 1960, the city where he currently lives. He writes poetry, short stories and drama. His work has appeared in print, on radio and on stage at the Edinburgh Festival.

RUTH THOMAS was born in Kent in 1967 and has lived in Edinburgh since 1985. Her first collection of short stories, *Sea Monster Tattoo* was published by Polygon in 1997.